HUMAN
SACRIFICES

HUMAN SACRIFICES

MARÍA FERNANDA AMPUERO

Translated from the Spanish by **Frances Riddle**

THE FEMINIST PRESS
AT THE CITY UNIVERSITY OF NEW YORK
NEW YORK CITY

Published in 2023 by the Feminist Press
at the City University of New York
The Graduate Center
365 Fifth Avenue, Suite 5406
New York, NY 10016

feministpress.org

First Feminist Press edition 2023

  This book is supported in part by an award from the National
Endowment for the Arts.

This book was made possible thanks to a grant from the New York State Council on the Arts with the support of Governor Kathy Hochul and the New York State Legislature.

First printing May 2023
Cover design by Sukruti Anah Staneley
Text design by Drew Stevens

Library of Congress Cataloging-in-Publication Data
Names: Ampuero, María Fernanda, author. | Riddle, Frances, translator.
Title: Human sacrifices / María Fernanda Ampuero ; translated from the
  Spanish by Frances Riddle.
Other titles: Sacrificios humanos. English
Description: First Feminist Press edition. | New York City : The Feminist
  Press, 2023.
Identifiers: LCCN 2022051083 (print) | LCCN 2022051084 (ebook) | ISBN
  9781558612983 (paperback) | ISBN 9781558612990 (ebook)
Subjects: LCSH: Ampuero, María Fernanda—Translations into English. |
  Capitalism—Fiction. | Working class women—Fiction. |
  Children—Fiction. | LCGFT: Short stories.
Classification: LCC PQ8220.41.M68 S2313 2023 (print) | LCC PQ8220.41.M68
  (ebook) | DDC 863/.7—dc23/eng/20221122
LC record available at https://lccn.loc.gov/2022051083
LC ebook record available at https://lccn.loc.gov/2022051084

PRINTED IN THE UNITED STATES OF AMERICA

CONTENTS

To Pablo

*Writing is also bestowing a blessing
on a life that was not blessed.*

—CLARICE LISPECTOR,
Too Much of Life

BIOGRAPHY

What a fool, she's insane, you might say, but I want you to see me living undocumented in a foreign country carefully counting the few bills I have left to pay my rent and buy a loaf of bread and a cup of black coffee. Desperation and the internet collide, mount each other, engender monstrous beasts, aberrations.

I go online to the Seeking Employment pages and post all the kinds of jobs that they might give someone like me. Cleaning, caretaking, washing, sewing, selling, handing out, filing, picking up, stacking, restocking, growing, greeting, watching. They call and immediately ask about my papers.

"I'm in the process of getting my residency."

"Call us when you have it."

Or:

"Papers in order?"

"Not yet."

"We don't hire illegals."

Over and over, every day.

Anxiety creeps up my neck like a cold, crinkly black insect with a stinger. Do you know the creature I'm talking about? It's hard to explain the feeling when it nests on your back. It's like dying but you're still alive. Like trying to breathe underwater. Like being cursed.

Under these circumstances, writing is the most useless thing in the world. It's a ridiculous skill, a dead weight, a kind of hubris. I'm a foreign scribe documenting a world that despises her.

One day after countless ads offering my services as caretaker, nanny, maid, cook and hearing, "Not without papers, we don't hire illegals," I decide to post something absurd.

Do you think that your life story is worthy of a book, but you don't know how to tell it? Call me! I'll tell your tale!

I didn't think the message, with its exclamation marks, would interest anyone.

An hour later my phone rang. Unknown number.

"I have a story that the world has to hear."

The guy was named Alberto. He said that he lived in a small town in the north, that he could pay whatever I was asking, that he couldn't give me more details over the phone, and that I'd have to go meet him the next day if I was interested in the job.

After a long silence, I asked for a lot of money because his voice frightened me, because I'd have to travel clear across a country that was not my own, and because I thought he would refuse to pay that amount to a stranger, not to mention a foreign stranger.

"I'll wire half the payment right now."

His tone was overfamiliar, which scared me. That friendliness older men sometimes extend and you don't know if it's because they see you as a dumb daughter, because they want to get their hands on you, or both.

When I first emigrated here, my boss at the internet café, the one who told me I reminded him of his little girl back home, tried to rape me inside one of the phone booths where other people like me cried over their dead or consoled their living. When I resisted, he bashed my head into the telephone. With my mouth full of blood, I turned around, screamed, and spit in his face.

I ran half-naked out into the recently washed street and no one called the police because in that neighborhood everyone knew that the police punished only undocumented people, not rapists.

My boss had his papers in order, so I'd be the one in trouble.

See me, see me. I run down the street wearing one shoe, my blouse torn open, my bra strap broken, skirt bunched up around my hips.

See me, see me. Shouting like I've just escaped an explosion, flames still blazing in my hair, the stench of scorched flesh, my teeth stained with black blood. I scream that I'm dying, that he's trying to kill me.

See my neighbors, silent, on the sides of the street. Watching the procession of Our Lady of the Foreign Women, a saint who receives no offerings, whom no one gives a shit about.

I cried in the shower as my blood tinged the water red like in the movies, and the next day I started to look for a new job. I didn't get paid for the days I'd worked at the internet café.

When this Alberto guy sent me the advance, a fortune, I had the urge to jump for joy, but something told me not to.

We undocumented immigrants have to hold our brightly colored bills close to our chests, warming them against our hearts, treating them as if they were our children. We give birth to them with a wrenching pain the body doesn't soon forget.

I thought about my options until my head hurt. I asked the woman who rented me a place to sleep in her living room, my only acquaintance in the city, my compatriot, and she told me that yes, it was dangerous, very dangerous in fact, but sleeping on the street would be worse.

"Look, honey, when you emigrate you know you're in for the worst, like going off to war. You don't emigrate if you're going to be scared of every little thing. Grit your teeth and clench your thighs shut and do what you have to do: you know it's already the first of the month."

That day, with the money Alberto sent me, I felt human for a few hours. I wired money home, I called my parents and told them to kiss my daughter for me, I went into a supermarket and bought meat and fresh fruit, I had coffee with milk on a café terrace like any normal woman.

Then fear sprayed me with its acid water. I scarfed down my dinner like a stray dog. I caught an overnight bus headed north. Somewhere along the way, I don't know what time, I fell asleep.

I dreamed that a turkey had gotten into my daughter's room and was pecking at the soft spot on her head. I immediately understood that the turkey was a demon and that demons feed on the pure thoughts of infants. I wanted to scream, but I didn't have a mouth. The screams echoed through my brain, everything inside shaking like a maraca, making my heart swell until I couldn't breathe.

I didn't have legs. I didn't have arms to pick up my baby and take her away from the turkey. I wasn't a person, I was an eye—an eye that cried the bloody milk of an infected nipple onto my daughter. The turkey turned around, looked at me. Its face was my face. It screamed: *Run.*

"Run!"

I was woken up by my own screams, and the woman sitting beside me gave me a dirty look and changed seats. *Stupid foreigner*, she thought. *They're so strange*, she thought. *I bet she's sick*, she thought. I disgusted her.

Waiting for me at the station was a man who wasn't Alberto but who, he said, was a "disciple of Master Alberto." He was old or looked it: toothless and so stooped that I was a full head taller. He wore a black shirt and pants and a kind of velvet cape with a hood that seemed out of place among all the people in puffer coats.

I considered saying I had to go to the bathroom, then buying a return ticket and putting the whole thing behind me, but I stayed because I wanted the other half of the payment. What had I come here for if not to make money? What had I come here for if not to try my luck? What had I come here for if not to survive no matter what?

Desperate women serve as meat for the grinder. Immigrant women are bones to be pulverized into animal fodder.

Unhardened bone. Pure cartilage. The soft spot on the head of the world.

I thought about my parents thousands of miles away, waiting for the wire transfer so they could start paying off my trip and feed my daughter. We knew all about loan sharks of course—that they're dangerous creatures who make everything easy until you're in a real bind and then they devour you alive—but we also knew that staying in the country would be even worse.

Our economy was dollarized, went to shit: every family had to sacrifice its best lamb.

We'd heard stories about emigrants who owed money receiving calls from ghastly voices saying they were watching their little daughter play in the park and your little girl is so cute with her pigtails, I bet she smells delicious, she's getting to be a big girl, isn't she? She's as pretty as a flower.

I rode for half an hour with the old man in a long black car. I was too scared to speak, and anyway it was like he wasn't even there, like a driver painted on a toy car. We left the town behind, the gas stations, the industrial complexes, and we drove down an abandoned side road until we reached some woods.

There, I discovered that my phone had no signal.

There, we reached Alberto's house.

It was almost pretty, a white stone cottage with a red roof and sunflowers growing along the front. To one side were rabbit hutches and a chicken coop and a well. There was a chimney with smoke billowing out and a brick barbecue grill.

I was reminded of those kids visiting the gingerbread house, who'd given in to the temptation of the sugar windows as a cannibal watched from inside, licking her lips.

Alberto came out to greet me flanked by two Dobermans. As a little girl I'd had a Doberman named Pacha who would eat flowers, leaves, and anything else she came across. She was friendly and docile until one day she wasn't. She snatched a sweet roll from my baby sister's right hand and took off two fingers along with it.

That afternoon my dad tied Pacha up, fed her, petted her smooth back like black silk, and then shot her in the head.

I watched it all from inside the house.

I asked Alberto if the dogs were vicious and he said yes.

Then I turned around to say goodbye to the old man but the car was already gone, with no sign it had been there at all.

For a few seconds Alberto and I stared at each other, sizing each other up.

See me, see me. Fragile as a chicken's neck. A foreign woman with a backpack on her back standing before a strange man with two fierce, enormous dogs in the most remote corner of a remote town in a remote country.

See me, see me. Tiny thing in a big world, a human sacrifice, nothing.

Here, no one would hear me scream.

Even if I shred my vocal cords, even if I shriek until I'm destroyed inside, no one will hear me. Only the trees, the beautiful winter sky, but under trees and beautiful skies the most horrifying things occur as they watch on, unfeeling, distant, selfish.

Women devoured by ants, no longer girls but composite sketches, dismembered dolls, charred and blackened, reduced to bones, punctured, decapitated, naked bodies with no pubic hair, skinned alive, babies wearing a single tiny white shoe, women who die of fright over what's being done to them, tied up with their own underwear, emptied out, raped to death, lacerated, fed to the worms and larvae, gnawed by human teeth, bruised, eyeless, eviscerated, purple, red, yellow, green, gray, drowned and eaten by fishes, bloodless, perforated, dissolved in acid, beaten beyond recognition.

All of them, each and every one, begged for god, man, or mother nature to help.

God doesn't love, men murder, and nature rains clean water down on the bloodied bodies, the sun bleaches their bones, a tree drops its leaves onto the unrecognizable face of someone's daughter, the earth sprouts glorious sunflowers that feed on the purple flesh of disappeared women.

If I try to run Alberto will release the dogs.

Who will tell my parents? Will anyone ever find me? Will my little girl grow up thinking that her mother abandoned her? Will the loan sharks forgive our debt?

See me. See me. Afraid to show my fear. If Alberto senses my terror, it could be the detonator, the spark that lights the fuse, the short circuit: *Why so nervous? Do I frighten you? I'll show you, you dirty whore, what fear really is.*

See me, see me. I feign composure and I smile. He doesn't return the smile.

I asked the dogs' names and he mumbled something I didn't catch, but I didn't dare to ask again. I learned very young never to bother an angry man, a drunk man, a strange man, a man.

I learned never to say that this mouth is mine because it never has been.

He went into the house and I followed him. Why?

An immigrant heart is a bird in the hand. I have mouths to feed.

I have to eat.

I have to be eaten.

When he locked the door, part of my body bristled and the other part turned to lead. My heart shrunk up like it had been vacuum sealed. My lips stuck to my gums. I swallowed glass. I could hardly breathe.

See me, see me. And hear me. I say to myself, *Nothing's wrong, silly girl, you'll see. You're going to hear this man's story and then he'll take you to the station, you'll get on the bus, and you'll sleep soundly. The girl will be able to get a new dress, Mom will cook shrimp stew, you and your whole body will fully exist. You'll exist, dummy, you'll exist.*

The house was dark inside and it smelled like old food, like something with cabbage cooked a long time ago that had fermented, like poor ventilation, like filth, like depravity. There was hardly any furniture or pictures or mirrors. It looked like an abandoned house, a hideout. I asked Alberto if I could use the phone and he told me that he hadn't paid his bill, so they'd cut his service. The electricity too.

I felt like I'd stepped on a landmine, the sound of the detonator echoed through my mind, *click.* I'd fallen into a trap, the kind that animals in the forest will gnaw off their own legs to free themselves from, bleeding to death as they run away. A burst of terror blinded me for a few seconds and when I opened my eyes, I looked to Alberto for some compassion, some apology, some understanding of the terror a foreign woman must feel here all alone, who knows where with who knows who.

There was none. Nothing.

How long do you have to pretend that everything's fine until you can admit that you're infinitely fucked and you know it? How long do you have to wait before casually reaching for an ashtray, a fire poker, a flower vase to smash over his head? How much caution can a cornered animal afford to exercise? What about a woman?

See me, see me: I practice my good manners before the beast's gaping maw, I'm graceful as a princess as I fall into the abyss, I swallow back the black bile and say, "Oh, okay, I just wanted to let everyone know I'm all right."

My mousy little voice disgusts me.

We sit at a rough wooden table. I take out my recorder, my notebook, and as he does something that I interpret as praying—eyes closed tight, arms wide, palms open—I look around. The walls have writing on them. Fat strokes of bright red paint with Bible verses:

Be zealous and repent!

As many as I love, I rebuke and chasten.

We have sinned! We have acted wickedly!

The end is near!

He will rise again!

My eyes fill with tears, but instead of running, screaming, kicking, saying, *What the fuck is that, crazy fucker, goddamn psycho, I'm leaving right this minute*, I take out a pack of tissues and pretend to blow my nose.

Suddenly, without warning and without lifting his head, he begins to speak as if to himself.

I hurriedly smash the record button.

His voice is monotone, flat as an incantation, like wood being sanded.

He began with his poor childhood in the city, marked by a hunger so blinding it drove him and his twin brother to hunt rats and pigeons so they'd have something to chew on besides pure misery, to quiet the monster living in their guts. They made up games using rocks and empty beer cans, had dreams of ice cream cones, toys, strawberries and sweet cream that ended when they woke up on their filthy mattress, the nightmare beginning all over again.

He spoke about the abuse, his father decimating his mother, his mother bleeding from everywhere, his mother crippled, his mother so devoted, his mother toothless, deaf in one ear.

His mother, full of sorrows.

He and his brother jacked each other off to keep from feeling. Then they beat each other's bodies, faces, genitals. They asphyxiated themselves with plastic bags; cut themselves with razor blades; pulled each other's fingernails off; shaved their heads, removing bits of scalp; gave themselves crooked, creepy tattoos with needles and ink; branded each other's skin.

Then they discovered glue, drugs, prostitution.

He told of how he and his brother, growing bigger, more manly, more sinister each day, made a pact to kill their father the next time he beat their mother. They fashioned knives from tin cans and sharpened sticks that they hid under their bed.

But the father never hit the mother again because he never came back.

He and his brother said goodbye to their childhood that day: the men of the house have no time for dreams.

He talked about how he was a recovering addict, that drugs had been the love of his life and he'd debased himself for them more than he could say. He'd consumed anything he could find. Until the incident with his mother.

The woman was very sick, but he and his brother decided to rob her, once again, of the few bills she received from the state and the medicine she took for the pain. They bought drugs, little bags of disgusting shit that they heated on a spoon and injected into their ruined arms. They fell asleep on a corner with the other junkies. They didn't dream. That night, alone, without her medication, racked with a pain so severe she let out howls from beyond the grave, shaking like a person possessed, biting her tongue, her eyes bulging from their sockets, her hands stiff as branches, their mother died.

They returned home, purple skies soaring above, dripping blood from their arms, singing sweet lullabies for dead babies. A neighbor had called an ambulance. When the paramedics arrived, they were like actors in a TV sitcom. Everything was hilarious to them, especially the expression of their dead mother with her jaw hanging open and her eyes wide. *Mom, how hysterical, what a funny face you're making, Mom.* They gave her hugs and kisses. Before the paramedics could remove her from the house, they locked themselves inside. *Why do these clowns want to take her away when she's perfectly happy? Mom, you're happier than ever, right?* As the police came to break down the door, they put their dead mother in a floral dress, danced around with her, stuck plastic flowers in her hair, moved her arms to make her shimmy seductively; they gave her a glass of wine and a cigarette. *That was the last time, Mommy,* they said to her. *Sorry about your pills, we promise not to do it again. But look how much better you are, you don't need them anymore. Dance, Mommy, dance.* Then their dead mother gripped their arms so tightly that they had purple bruises for weeks. Alberto rubbed his wrist as if it still hurt, and after a long silence he spoke in a wisp of a voice.

"She looked at us and said that if we ever got high again, she'd come and kill us."

They sobered up instantly and realized they'd been profaning their mother's corpse.

"Even today I can't explain how she grabbed our arms. It might've been rigor mortis, I don't know. From that moment on I completely changed my life, I never shot up any more shit; I had to get away from the dealers, from everyone I knew. I gave up the apartment and came out here to the country. The fresh air cleansed me and I found the Good Word. Or the Good Word found me, I don't know. My brother also found the Word, but a darker, more dangerous one."

I felt brave enough to finally ask a question.

"Where is he now?"

He sighed.

"It's hard for me to talk about him. Maybe tomorrow."

Then a horrifying grimace contorted his face, like he was in overwhelming pain, and he transformed into another person entirely. His eyes were two bright red coals burning in their sockets. He growled with his mouth so wide I could see the holes where his teeth should have been, the black stains of his cavities, his pointy tongue.

"Tell the slut that I'm right here. Tell her about me, you son of a bitch. You brought this piece of shit foreigner to hear our story, now tell it, but tell it right, brother, don't leave anything out."

He looked me in the eye for the first time all day.

"What's wrong, you cow? You want me to tell you the truth, what my coward brother isn't able to admit? You want me to talk about Our Lord of the Night? You think you have the fucking right to enter our home? Foreign trash, disgusting whore, why did you come here? To take. That's what you're here for. That's what you all come for. You come to take what's ours. You want everything, everything: our money, our stories, our dead, our ghosts. You'll see what the Lord and I have in store for you and all the other whores who come to infest our streets."

The dogs barked frenziedly.

"You know what my dogs feed on? On foreign sluts like you."

See me, see me. I stand up with impossible speed, I move backward until I bump against the wall, I cover my face with my hands, I bite my fist to keep the deafening scream inside me from escaping. A white bolt of terror courses through me. I feel my frantic heartbeat crashing against the walls. I moan, I beg please, please, please. I say that I have a daughter, Alberto, have mercy on me.

"Sit down, slut. Of course you have children, you people squeeze out babies like pigs, you have so many kids that soon there will be no more pure-blooded people left in the fucking world. We'll kill you all."

He spit on the floor.

By that late hour the only light came from the amber glare of the fireplace that projected giant shadows onto the walls, the red words shouting: *Repent! The end is near! Repent!*

I watched as he moved toward me.

See me, see me. Blinded by fright, my eyes huge and clouded, dizzy, my brain firing sparks like a sharpening stone.

See me, see me. Forcing myself to think the only rational thing, *You're dreaming, this isn't real, wake up, wake up now.*

See me, see me. When he's so close I can smell his breath like sulfur and decay, I piss myself, I can't speak. I make guttural sounds, squeals, as if instead of a person I were a rabbit still alive between a wolf's jaws. My voice comes out stunned, barely a puff of air.

"Alberto, I'm begging you, think of your mother, Alberto."

See him, see him. He goes silent as if he's been doused with a fire extinguisher. He lowers his head, apologizes.

"You're right, I'm sorry. It's just that the grief is still very fresh, and I don't always feel like myself."

By the time he stood up and moved away from me, it was fully night, the darkest night imaginable, the kind of night from back when the world and its creatures didn't yet exist. He lit some red candles and placed them around the room. We'd been sitting for several hours, without water, without food, without going to the bathroom.

"Alberto? Are you okay?"

"Of course, woman, of course."

"Alberto? Could you please take me to the station? You know, I'm thinking it might be better to leave it for later . . . ? Or, well, I want to go back . . ."

"Impossible, I don't have a car and there are no buses running at this hour."

I picked up my backpack and hugged it to my chest. In a whisper, I asked where the bathroom was. I was soaked with urine and I was on my period. Bloody wetness ran down my legs to my shoes. A bonfire of terror raged in my gut.

When I opened the bathroom door the smell shot out like a wild animal, hungry, toxic. It assaulted my nostrils and forced me backward. It smelled like pure ammonia, like death, like pus, like rotting blood, like a gas leak. In the red candlelight, the floor, the toilet, the walls, the sink, the tub were one brownish stain that seemed alive, organic. It took everything I had not to vomit. The stench coated me from the inside out like I'd been drenched in sewer water, and the soles of my feet stuck to something dark and gummy on the floor.

I would've preferred to go outside, among the trees, but I thought of the dogs, the darkness, of him and this so-called Lord of the Night.

Half of the bathroom door was etched glass. I squatted and tried to avoid staining myself further with urine and blood as I pulled down my pants, my underwear, the soaked pad, trying to not touch anything and stay clean. I saw the shadow of his head looming on the other side of the door. It didn't move. I heard a voice whispering, "No, no," and another, that different, monstrous voice, saying, "Stupid fucking fag, you can't do anything right, you idiot, why did you bring her here then?"

I imagined him breaking the glass, unlocking the door, raping and killing me on that repugnant floor swirling with things that looked like hairs, that looked like blood clots.

I wanted to tell him to stop watching me, to shout, *What's wrong with you*, but I didn't say a word. I looked for some way to escape, but the bathroom had only a tiny barred window.

Beside the bathroom was a bedroom that Alberto had made up for me. It had a small bed, a nightstand, and a rocking chair in which sat an enormous old teddy bear. There was a window covered by a sheer curtain, and through it I could see the shadow of the two dogs, one beside the other, standing on their hind legs, as tall as me. I could hear them panting heavily, like they were hunting.

Alberto placed red candles on the little table and the room filled with the evil glow of an old church, the same glare that falls on the faces of little girls as they kneel on dusty prayer stools, begging for forgiveness for things they didn't know were sins.

On the wall was more large red writing: *Repent!* and over the bed hung a cross with a Christ bathed in blood.

"This was my mother's room. You'll be comfortable here."

He closed the door, took a few steps, and then returned.

"Don't forget to lock the door."

See me, see me. Alone in a freezing room that smells of mildew and neglect, separated by only a thin door from a man who threatened to feed me to his dogs. I try not to make any noise. I carefully push the bed against the door and climb onto it without taking my eyes off the lock.

See me, see me. A foreign woman alone is like a fawn is like a baby is like a hangnail easily bitten off, chewed up, and spit out. In the middle of the woods, inside a house of horrors, listening to the barking of rabid dogs, I cry like I've never cried in my life.

Don't look at me. It will only make you angry. What a fool, she's insane, you'll say.

My brain takes over: *You have to save yourself.* Very slowly, glancing repeatedly back at the door, I open the closets and drawers. There must be something here I can use to defend myself. I jump as I pass the rocking chair with the bear. The thing seems to come alive, its eyes glistening in the red candlelight, its paws reaching out to me.

See me, see me. Paralyzed with fear like there's a poisonous snake at my feet. In one drawer I find passports, blue ones, red ones, green ones, of girls from all over the world. Like mine, almost all of the passports are the first ones they've ever had. They smile through clenched teeth. The way I smile too.

I take out the recorder and say their names as if I were praying a rosary. I repeat their birthdays, their nationalities, the dates they arrived in the country; I describe them. I press each passport against my pounding heart.

See me, see me. And hear me. I pronounce their names as best I can. Awa. Fátima. Julie. Wafaa. Bilyana.

See them, see them. They were also fools, insane.

They were also immigrants.

I close the drawer with the passports and in another one I find toothbrushes, address books, deodorants, lotions, fake nails, eyelash curlers, glasses, prayer books, the Quran, little cards with pictures of virgins and saints, books, photographs of little boys and girls, of people smiling in front of a house, a very old woman surrounded by dozens of adults, teenagers, and children.

In a third drawer I find locks of hair: dark curly hair, straight hair dyed red, blond hair like dry grass, hair that belonged to someone, that shone under the sun on the head of a living woman.

Terrified, I take a few steps back and trip over the rocking chair. The bear falls, I fall. On the floor the bear and I look like two dying animals, bleeding out after the hunt.

The dogs know it. They sniff frantically at the scent of blood in the air, they lick their chops in anticipation, their growling, drooling faces fill the window.

I lie on the floor looking at the bear, who returns my gaze. I find a flimsy wooden plank under the bed, I wield it as if instead of an immigrant I were, I don't know, a sorceress, an Amazon warrior. I imagine a flurry of blows, I picture Alberto floundering in a sea of blood, brains, and teeth, begging for mercy.

Every hour that passes is an eon, and in that eon the teddy bear and I wait for horrible things to happen, we grow old, we cry silently. The early hours bring a storm. Now it's the noise of the dogs, but also the wind like a pack of hounds, the lightning and thunder, the tree branches scraping furiously at the window.

See me, see me. I grab the dirty bear by the foot and place him next to my body. Side by side, the bear and I are the most pathetic army in the world, barricaded against evil behind a twin-size bed.

I pray, petting the bear's fur with my sweaty palms, and I think the bear is praying too.

When we hear noise on the other side of the door, the bear and I strain our ears, open our eyes wide, futilely, in a darkness that has long since swallowed the candlelight. We whimper with fear.

The door handle moves up and down, up and down, up and down. Alberto who isn't Alberto knocks with a monstrous rage. I think he's going to beat down the door.

"Open up, slut, open up, I have a job for you, isn't that what you wanted? To come here to work? Open the fucking door, fucking foreign bitch, open up right now."

I hug the bear and cry. I beg, "Alberto, please."

I hear Alberto's voice, asking someone to calm down, to show some respect. He begins to shout a prayer and cry for his mother.

"Our Father who art in heaven, hallowed be thy name, thy kingdom come, thy will be done . . . Mother, please, Mother."

The other voice, which seems to come from Alberto's guts, tells him that praying is useless, that the slut is already dead, and why did he bring her here if it wasn't for the ceremony.

Alberto continues to pray.

"Deliver us from evil, deliver us from evil. Mother, I beg you, Mother. No more."

Suddenly a terrible wail, unbearable, inhuman: the howl of someone who can't believe what they are seeing because what they are seeing isn't possible.

The teddy bear and I imagine the scene: the hammer sinking into a face, the nose smashed into the back of the head, the brutal crunch of a cranium hitting the floor, the jelly of the eyes exploding under the pressure of a thumb, the spurt of blood from the ripped-open neck, the hoarse death rattle of the final gasp.

Then nothing else. No Alberto, no madman pounding on the door, nothing. A silence that is like darkness: an open mouth that doesn't speak.

I hug the bear tighter. I give him a kiss on his dusty nose. We sit there for ages, curled up against the bed, him with his bear's eyes and me with my foreign woman's eyes, staring off into space, waiting for who knows what.

When I stand up I realize that the dogs have been silent for a long time. I peek out the window, they're not there. I look at the predawn sky. It's the most beautiful sky I've ever seen. The stars shine like they never do in the city, omnipotent, excessive. I remember someone once told me that the stars we see have been dead for a long time, and I think that maybe the disappeared women might also shine on like that, with that same blinding light, making it easier to find them.

I hug the bear and thank him. I pet his furry face and I notice that it's as wet as mine. I open the window with infinite caution and fall like a newborn baby out into the starry night of the world.

See me, see me. Fleeing like an animal in shock over its unexpected survival, an animal that doesn't look back because no one is chasing it, taking long strides and kicking up dust and bathing in it as if it were glitter. Alive. A live animal.

The breeze dries my tears as I run toward the purple crack of the horizon. The day crossing the black border of the night.

See them, see them. Lined up along the side of the road, like shadows, they watch me rush past and they smile, my sisters in migration. They whisper: *Tell our story, tell our story, tell our story.*

See her, see her. The pale reflection of a gleaming head and a flowered dress blessing me like all mothers: making the sign of the cross with her hands.

BELIEVERS

There was an alleyway out back where the sun never shined and a thick slime, almost a living creature, slippery as a frog's back, formed on the ground and walls. I discovered it the day the strike began, drunk on freedom because it was a Tuesday and on Tuesdays I had two straight hours of math followed by PE, my two worst enemies.

That morning we arrived at school to find it closed because of the strike. My parents took me to my grandma's, and on an impulse, the kind that leaves you with one foot in the air and the other on the ground, I decided to help her with the tea roses, which were plump and pink and full of thorns like she was, but I quickly realized she only cut flowers to keep from cutting the head off of some person. She looked like a butcher in her black garden gloves, a cigarette hanging from the corner of her mouth.

I went into the shed and rummaged through Grandpa's tools, organized them by size, stripped several cables to reveal the gleaming copper inside, and made myself a ridiculous bracelet. Grandpa would've shown me some magic trick or given me detailed descriptions of the currency he'd collected from around the world. But Grandpa was dead because, as my dad always said, god takes his favorites first.

After a while, bored, I started running around outside the house. My black school shoes made a sound like a bag of marbles being spilled on the sidewalk. I liked it.

There was an alleyway out back where the sun never shined, and that was where I slipped on a sickly sweet, furry slime like a green rat and I fell flat on my back and lay there, my skirt hiked up, me and my white panties looking up at the sky. I felt like crying, not from pain, but from fear. It was the first time I'd ever thought about my own death, and death was exactly that: being alone in an alleyway where the sun never shines and no one, ever, will come looking for you. It was also the first time I realized I'd have to live with myself and my insufferable, irritating, insistent voice for the rest of my life.

After a little while Patafría walked by carrying the dirty clothes basket. She was startled at first, but then she saw it was me. She stood me up and wiped me off and frowned at the stains on my white panties and she said, "You look like an idiot, child, lying there." We went into the kitchen; she cleaned my legs and face with a damp cloth that smelled like the butcher shop. Don't cry, she said, your grandmother doesn't like crybabies.

What Patafría really meant was that my grandmother didn't like anything except cards, herself, and nicotine. I wasn't crying, but when she mentioned it I felt like I should cry: *I'm going to die, I saw myself dead, and I missed myself, myself and all the things I planned to do with myself. I'm going to die, Patafría, do you understand?* Something frozen like my own death skittered up my body. I stopped when Patafría raised a bony finger, the color of hot chocolate, and wagged it in front of my nose. No crying.

Patafría was the woman who worked for my grandma. Her real name was María, like my grandma, but she'd changed it because it was too horrifying to have the same name. Patafría had a daughter, Marisol, who turned up the day the strike began.

I was shocked that so close to my world there lived a girl my age and I didn't know her. I didn't have many friends. Why hadn't Patafría's daughter ever come to my birthday, or the other way around: Why hadn't they ever invited me to Patafría's daughter's birthday? Why hadn't they ever brought her over to swim in the pool? How hadn't I known about her? Who did Marisol live with if Patafría lived at my grandma's house? I couldn't ask my grandmother, and I couldn't ask Patafría either. So I asked Marisol. She shrugged her shoulders, took me by the hand, and led me to the alley where the sun never shined.

There was something strange about Marisol, although I couldn't say what it was. She never gave a straight answer, stood with her mouth hanging open for too long; she would scratch her head nonstop and sometimes she would fall silent, as if listening to someone who was giving her very confusing but very important instructions. But she smiled a lot, and it was fun to have another girl at Grandma's house. It wasn't a big deal that she always had her tongue hanging out or laughed too loud or couldn't answer questions or clapped at planes when they flew over. It was impossible to teach her to play cards, so I showed her the sound like marbles when we ran past the alleyway. We ran and ran and finally, exhausted, we decided to become best friends. She spit in her hand and held it out to me. I understood that I should do the same. We shook hands and the spit sealed our friendship.

Around that time the Believers moved into Grandma's house. There were two of them, a tall one and a short one, and those were the names we gave them, Tall Believer and Short Believer, because their real names, although they repeated them slowly, breaking up the syllables, were impossible to pronounce. The Believers explained how they went around to different countries talking about how good it was to be a Believer. Poor countries like this one, my grandma said, they come to stuff that religion of theirs down the throats of poor people with the promise of salvation and other idiotic ideas. Grandma didn't care about faith one way or the other; she was just interested in the money the Believers were willing to pay to sleep in the storage shed she'd fixed up but which still had bats in the rafters and which Dad said no one should ever rent, even for free.

The Believers were out all day. I imagined them walking around that city in flames, paralyzed by the strike, like they were tourists to the end of days, fascinated by the dark-skinned men killing each other. We couldn't tell when they were home or not because the door was always closed and they put newspapers over the windows so that no one could look inside. They came into the kitchen every once in a while to ask for cold water. They never accepted anything else. Patafría felt sorry for them; she said it was horrible they had to live in that hellhole without any ventilation or comforts to speak of, despite the fact that her own room was no more than a tiny cave that barely fit her rickety bed and an overturned box where she set her toothbrush and her Bible.

When they came to ask for water she always offered them some food or a pitcher of juice, but they said no, no to everything. She also tried to give them palo santo to keep away the mosquitoes that were eating them alive, but they said no and she would stand there with the tray in her hands looking at them with admiration, maybe even love, as they went back to their rattrap.

What did the Believers eat? No one knew. They refused Patafría's offerings and they couldn't make food in the shed. They once left the door cracked open and I saw them naked, pouring pitchers of ice water on each other. Then they lay down on the bed and stared at the ceiling, wet, their tongues out, panting, until I heard Patafría call me to lunch. I didn't tell anyone what I'd seen.

I was fascinated by them. The Believers were beautiful, blond as Baby Jesus; they surely must be kind. My parents had warned me over and over about strangers on the street, about drifters who stole little children, about beggars, but never about men with eyes that were so blue, so green they were almost transparent. They had to be good.

The Believers gave Patafría some beautiful books and even though they were in another language, they had very entertaining drawings of what looked like aliens, and a party with animals and people and aliens. You could make up incredible stories based on the pictures in the Believers' books, but Patafría didn't even open them. She just said thank you and left the books sitting in a corner of the kitchen. It made me sad they hadn't given me one.

What I didn't understand was how Grandma could have the Believers living in her house if Dad said they were sinners, but I once heard Dad say to Mom that it was better they were there so Grandma could make some money off of them and that, in any case, if you didn't have to listen to them talk about salvation and the planet where all the chosen ones would go, they were fairly inoffensive. Dad said that given the situation the country was in, with the strike and all that, it was a good thing for Grandma to have two white guys at her house.

That day, the first day of the strike, Marisol and I, already best friends forever, discovered a hole in the wall through which we could see into the Believers' room. We quickly got bored because there was nothing interesting going on. The Believers had no appliances, no decorations or photographs, not a single thing besides their white shirts, their black pants, and a little suitcase for each of them. Then suddenly Marisol screamed and covered her mouth with her hands.

"What? What did you see?"

"A little boy," she said.

The Believers couldn't possibly have a little boy in their room.

I peeked inside and burst out laughing. All I saw was a pile of clothes on the chair. I told Marisol that she was a dummy and she hit me and I hit her back and we were mad at each other for an hour until I realized that if I lost her I'd be all alone. I went over to her and, I don't know why, I told her about the time my grandma found a cat and a litter of kittens in her yard and she picked up the kittens and put them in a plastic bag, then tied it tight with a triple knot and stomped on it with her orthopedic shoes. Then she mixed a few gray baggies of poison into a can of tuna and fed it to the mother. I got really serious so that Marisol would understand that my grandma was dangerous.

"Do you know the sound a kitten skull makes under a grandma's shoe? No? Well, I do."

It got hot and we went inside. There were cartoons on at that time of day. I took off my shoes and got on Grandma's bed. I told Marisol to do the same. When Grandma came in and found the two of us head to head, watching *Woody Woodpecker*, she got furious and told Patafría to take her daughter back to the kitchen.

Then she ordered her to change the bedspread, the pillowcases, and the sheets.

From that day onward I ate in the kitchen with Patafría and Marisol. There was no convincing me to sit with my grandma, even when she threatened to have my father beat me. From that day on I became, in her eyes, a spoiled, ungrateful brat.

Outside, the strike was increasingly violent. Grandma's friends came over to tell her that so-and-so's employees had taken over the company and had strung him up above the machinery while they all applauded. Ungrateful beasts, murderers. They told her about a family where the cook had poisoned the soup and how all of a sudden the cook and her children lived in the family's mansion, swam in their pool, and wore all their name-brand clothes. Other ladies stopped in to say goodbye because they were leaving the country. They cried.

"They're massacring us, María. Get out while you can."

Patafría cried too. She said that the river was choked with bodies full of bullet holes and that every morning at dawn the mothers of the murdered men would throw crosses into the water.

That river's not a river; it's death, death water.

The police went into the working-class neighborhoods and raped the dead men's mothers and daughters and sisters and grandmothers. Then they took everything of value and burned the houses down. They left the women half-naked, bloodied, lying on the ground.

Sometimes the tangy smell of gunpowder and tear gas would reach Grandma's house and we had to rush to shut the windows. We heard gunshots all day and all night.

Mom and Dad didn't come back. They were afraid that if they left the factory the workers would take over, as had happened with their friends' factories, so they brought in mattresses and a cookstove and camped out in the office so that, as Dad said, they could protect what Grandpa had worked so hard for. One day Grandma went to take them the shotgun and when she came back she looked much older, as if instead of having gone to the factory she'd gone to hell and back. What had she seen along the way? Her clothes were torn and there was mud in her hair.

For the first time she called Patafría by her real name.

"María, you're not going to betray us, are you? We've treated you like family, we've given you everything you needed, I even let you bring your daughter here when your husband and your sister joined the strike. You love us, don't you, María?"

Marisol and I became obsessed with the Believers; we

thought that they would save the country from the strike and then we'd all be happy. In the movies, men who looked like them always saved the planet.

We named the little boy Marisol said she saw but I thought was a pile of clothes Miguelito, and every day we made up new adventures for him. Miguelito flew to outer space, fought giants, traveled to the future and married us, inherited millions, went on safari. Miguelito did it all, but he always got into trouble. We died laughing as we swooped in to save Miguelito and humanity.

Our friendship was like love, a wonder that grew and grew.

Sometimes we kissed like on the telenovelas. I put my lips on her lips and we breathed. I liked the salty smoke of her breath more than candy and I wanted to stay there, mouth to mouth, forever. I rubbed her curls and she untied my ponytail to make my long hair dance against my face. Wearing a pillowcase and one of Grandpa's ties, we got married. Sometimes I wore the tie, sometimes she did, but we always ended up with our hands and lips pressed together, so close we looked like conjoined twins.

Every night Marisol waited for Patafría to fall asleep, then snuck into bed with me. Sleepless, fluttering with excitement, we told each other stories we already knew or invented new ones. It was a beautiful thing to be able to amaze someone, to make them laugh, to scare them, to be, for a little while, the same person.

It was a beautiful thing to tell Marisol stories until she fell asleep with her lips parted and her breath that smelled like a swamp, like mangroves, like mine.

One night we heard a wail, like a little kid crying, or

maybe a cat in heat. We went downstairs like two shadows and Marisol peeked through the hole in the Believers' wall. She turned to me and in her face I saw horror, more horror than can be put into words, more horror than one little girl can bear. I wanted to look, but she wouldn't let me. She hugged me and I heard her heart pounding, an animal about to be gutted.

We ran into the backyard and she told me that the Believers were biting the little boy. I thought she must be confused. I went back by myself and peeked through the hole. Tall Believer was wiping his mouth and Short Believer was tying up a garbage bag.

I laughed at Marisol.

"It was a chicken, dummy; they were eating chicken."

She was crying and shaking like a leaf as she went back to bed with her mom.

The next morning we were woken up by shouting in the street. Someone was calling for María. Her husband had been killed, and her sister too, along with half their neighborhood. Her mother had been badly injured, and all the houses had been burned down.

María, Marisol, my grandma, and I, one beside the other, stared at this woman who had crossed the city to bring the news, her brains boiling, her knees weak, and her jaw clenched like a person standing before the firing squad. The woman left and María fell to the floor. Grandma bent down to console her. With María curled into a ball and my grandma covering her with her large body, it wasn't clear which one of them was releasing that savage, wounded, animal wail. Maybe it was both of them at the same time: the cry of two women devastated by pain.

Marisol and I threw ourselves to the floor as well, one on top of the other, and the four of us lay there like that, two women and two girls screaming and crying, who knows how long.

María got up to go find her mother. Before leaving she asked my grandma to care for Marisol as if she were her own granddaughter, and Grandma promised she would. María said it again and Grandma put her cross necklace against her mouth. She swore to god. Marisol tried to follow Patafría, but Grandma caught the girl in her grave-digger's arms. I remembered the kittens that Grandma had separated from their mother, the sound of those tiny skulls, the final whimpers.

Days passed and Grandma got out of bed less and less until she stopped getting up at all. She called for Marisol to bring her coffee and cigarettes, to rub her feet and comb her hair. Marisol was always marching up and down the stairs with new orders from Grandma and so it was hard to play with her. I promised her that when my parents came back, we would take them, her and María, to live with us at our house.

As often as they could, my parents sent a trust-worthy messenger to let Grandma know they were all right. But one day the messages stopped coming. There were rumors that not a single business owner had been left alive, that they had been rounded up and left to starve, that some had been thrown from the skyscraper windows and their bodies had shattered like glass, that the industrial areas and downtown had been burned to the ground, that the bodies, by the hundreds, were attract-ing seagulls, rats, cats, and dogs from miles around. I thought about my parents and about animals eating their faces.

One afternoon the Believers came home with two little boys, and the next day with two more. The kids were starving, dirty, and confused. They looked like they'd been wandering alone for days. Grandma heard sounds and asked us about them. We lied and told her it was some beggars wanting bread or coins, and she told us not to let them in for anything in the world, that those starving wretches would kill their own mother over a rotten potato, that they would rape us and then eat us alive.

The Believers spread sheets on the floor of their room and the little boys slept there. Grandma stopped asking about the noises because she stopped talking entirely. Marisol and I cleaned her the best we could and fed her some of the meals we scraped together from the few items left in the pantry, a bit of rice, some tuna, tomato sauce.

Marisol wouldn't go near the Believers; she was still convinced that they ate people, and every morning she would peek in to make sure the little boys were still whole. After a few days she stopped checking. The Believers, she told me, treated the boys very well; they let them lie in their beds, took pictures of them, hugged them, gave them chocolate, and had them kiss one another on the mouth like we kissed each other. I convinced myself that I didn't hear them crying at night, that I didn't hear them shouting no and calling for their mamas. I must've made it all up, imagined those cries, that was the only possible explanation. The Believers were the good guys. The Believers were the only good guys left in the world.

WHISTLE

Mom never told me scary stories.

She told me stories about everything else: trips to the beach in the family van, her brothers' friends always at the house, sitting at the table in shifts, eating, talking, and stinking like pirates, the bags and baskets bursting with oranges, onions, tomatoes, shrimp, lemons, eggs, rice, crabs, fish, mangos, live chickens, which Grandpa brought home to feed the ravenous pack of hounds that were his offspring. She told me everything, down to the last detail. The tastes, smells, textures of her childhood, the first business she started when she was just a teenager, the stand she set up to sell bruised bananas that couldn't be sold for export. She never shut up about that, maybe because it was her first and last paying job, the first and last time that money passed through her hands. After that it was different: it was always Dad's. Money you've earned yourself has a different weight; it feels crisper, you pull it from your purse with a flourish and spread it across the counter, faceup, patting it like the head of a well-behaved child.

I know how she made a table out of banana crates

painted red and how she arranged the bunches of bananas tied with colorful ribbon—like a little girl's hair. I know she sometimes swapped bananas for things: songbooks, records, fashion magazines, mascara, a music box she kept the rest of her life. I know she loved being that child entrepreneur. I know that she used the money to buy chocolate, perfume. I know that her brothers stole her chocolate and ate it and that they sprayed her perfume on themselves to make their girlfriends jealous. I know that Mom's mom would hit her but not her brothers. I know that one time on the banana plantation they cut down some trees and out fell an orphaned baby monkey like a ripe fruit and Mom's dad brought him home and raised him like another child, eating, playing, and sleeping alongside them, until he became a teenage monkey and started masturbating in front of guests. They released him back into the trees, but the next day they found him dead in a hammock, like a tiny person taking a nap.

I know that when Mom met Dad she was dressed up like a soldier, with tall boots and tasseled hat, because she'd marched in a parade. I know that when Mom was little, her mom wasn't watching a gigantic pot of milk on the stove and that Mom was playing, exploring, and gallons and gallons of boiling milk spilled on her, her little dress stuck to her body, fused with her skin, and that, not knowing what to do, Mom's mom pulled the dress off her and with it ripped off the tender flesh of her little chest and that the pain was so bad, so bad, and she was so panicked at seeing her destroyed chest that she tried to jump out the window into a little stream that ran beside the house and that, to stop her, her mom grabbed her by her raw chest and she fainted from the pain. I know that the scars, that old lady's skin on a young woman, were something she was ashamed of her entire life. I know that Mom's mom set fire to the rats' nests and then blocked them off with rocks and that Mom, at night, would go around trying to cure the charred rats with menthol.

Mom told these and many, many more stories, but never a scary story. I was obsessed with scary stories because I knew they existed, that they had to. Dad had always lived in the city and some of the stories he told me would come into my head, without warning, at night when I went to sleep. One was about his friend Jo, who died in an accident, and that certain nights, especially when there was a full moon, Jo would come to his window and invite him out to play. The other was a night of strange sounds, like something with hooves, coming from his room. He went upstairs and found dark stains and burn marks on the wood floor, now scratched up, with sawdust everywhere.

I knew Mom, who had spent so much time in the country at her grandma's house, must have some even better stories. Or similar. Or worse. But some kind of scary story. I believed every word of Dad's stories so I was certain that evil existed and, since it existed, Mom had to have encountered it.

Finally she told her story one terrible night, the night my puppy died.

The neighbors had abandoned a little puppy without food or water and, after a few days hearing her yelp and feeding her bread soaked in milk that she devoured, Dad decided to go over and rescue her. It was crazy because my parents always said I couldn't have a dog, then all of a sudden the cutest little puppy in the world showed up at our house looking like a stuffed animal with two eyes like black marbles. The dog could fit entirely in the palm of Dad's hand, and she fell asleep there after licking his fingers. It was so exciting to have a pet and also to see my dad so animated, like he finally belonged to me and my mom and not to the streets, to other people.

That night we went to have dinner at my grandparents' and, of course, I took the little dog and, of course, I tied a red bow around her neck. I put a bowl of water down for her and there she went, wagging her tiny tail, wearing that bow bigger than she was. A little while later we saw her lying on her back, her tongue hanging out, grunting and with yellow foam coming out of her mouth. Dad's mom had put out rat poison all over the kitchen and the puppy ate some. That's what did it. She suffered for a few seconds, then died right in front of my eyes, which Mom tried in vain to cover: her lips pulled open to show her tiny teeth, the red ribbon like a hemorrhage on the floor, her little legs stiff. We'd saved her from her suffering next door only to kill her. Yes, my family had killed her. I'd killed her. That night, in bed, after begging me to stop crying, saying that I was going to make her cry, Mom started to tell me her scary story.

I'll never know why she chose that particular moment to tell me about the Whistler. It would've been the perfect opportunity to tell me about bright colors and vacations and ice cream with chocolate sprinkles, but that's not what she did.

Instead she started talking about a dog she'd had,

Wolf, a large, wise mutt who could understand and empathize with human emotions. Wolf was, Mom said, almost a person. She'd had a litter of eight puppies that were adorable creatures but, and this was the horrible part, their cuteness couldn't save them: they'd died of one illness after another, week after week. Not a single one lived beyond six months old. Wolf went wild with grief, searching for her babies all around the house, whining in the corner where she'd given birth, sniffing under the furniture and placing her enormous snout on Mom's skirt, staring up with her huge caramel-colored eyes as if asking, *Where are they?* As if asking for some explanation. Mom, just as sad as Wolf was over the puppies' deaths, decided to take the dog out to the country, to her grandma's house, to grieve.

Her grandma's house was raised on stilts and built out of canes so old they'd turned gray, the kind of rickety shack you see on the side of the highway when you're going from one nice place to the next. Mom would wax poetic when describing it, like it was the house of a fairytale grandmother, but I knew it was all a fantasy. The places you were happy always seem beautiful in your memory. It was, in reality, a precarious construction typical of the farmworkers in the area: an opulence of rotten wood, insects, and tin, without a toilet, running water, or electricity. Mom's grandma lived there alone because her husband had taken off with another woman when Mom was a little girl. That's where Mom turned up one day with the dog who'd lost all her puppies and a suitcase.

Mom's grandma was a fat, happy, loving old lady who let her get away with anything. Mom would sleep late, go back and forth to the beach all day, bringing back seashells and wildflowers as presents. She ate whenever she pleased and as much as she wanted, she rode the horse bareback, wore shorts or nothing at all, drank beer, smoked menthol cigarettes, and stayed up until late at night listening to her grandma's hilarious stories or to the soap operas they picked up on the transistor radio.

Her grandma worked a little plot of land where she made her living keeping chickens, some sheep, the horse, and a cow that was as calm, fat, and gullible as she was. Mom had been assigned certain chores: to go buy fish so fresh it was still flipping its tail in the bag on the way home, to milk the cow and skim the cream so that her grandma could whip it into white butter, to feed the animals, to collect the still-warm eggs—like they'd been boiled—and help her grandma make delicious, fluffy bread with those same eggs.

It was a self-sufficient world, a world free of fear, a happy world. Which is to say that Mom and her grandma were self-sufficient, free of fear, and happy.

The story, the night my puppy was poisoned, could have, should have, stopped at that point. Mom, her grandma, and her dog living in a joyous and uncomplicated matriarchy, free of constraints, their savage cackles over some joke about farts, sex, or the stupidity of men ringing out through the night black as a wolf's mouth, unblemished by electricity or neighbors.

Yes, the story should've stopped there. But Mom kept going.

One stormy night—the kind that in the country they call a water lashing, because it looks like the rain is lashing the world—Mom's grandma told her about the Whistler. She'd been trying to warn her for a while, but it was now urgent: a girl from the neighboring town, the sixth girl from the area that year, had disappeared a few days prior— "She was a free spirit, like you, baby," Mom's grandma said—and everyone was certain that all of the girls who had disappeared had been whistled at by the Whistler.

Mom curled up beside her grandma and thought about the missing girls; about herself going missing; about a black shadow, muzzled by darkness, creeping through the black night as the people who love you light matches in an attempt to find you until they tire of burning their finger-tips with the useless flames and stop searching. Mom's grandma became serious and begged her if she ever heard a whistle not to peek out the window for anything in the world, explaining that sometimes girls looked out of curi-osity, out of boredom, out of loneliness or love.

"Even if you think it's me, even if it sounds exactly like my whistle, even if you hear my voice telling you to open the window, to hand me something, that I had an accident—don't look out the window, my little girl. Even if you hear your father's voice or your mother's or some-one you love, the love of your life, your future children. Even if it orders you to look out the window, if it threat-ens you, begs you, pleads, promises you all the riches in the world, even if it says your name over and over again. Please, promise me that if you hear the Whistler, you won't look outside."

"What happens if you look?" Mom asked.

"Things too terrible to mention to a girl, baby. Prom-ise me that you won't look ever, promise me."

"Granny, did you ever hear the Whistler?"

She didn't answer.

So Mom promised and, even though she wanted to ask more questions, she didn't ask because her grandma had warned her that talking too much about the Whistler might attract him. Mom was terrified for the rest of the night, listening to the frantic heartbeat of her beloved grandmother, who also couldn't sleep until morning.

A few months later, Mom's dad went out to the country to get her, saying she had to come home and finish school. Then she could do as she pleased. Mom sobbed, her grandma sobbed, but Mom's dad gave her the only reason she couldn't deny.

"Baby girl, come home; you're the only one in that house who loves me."

Mom loved her father much more than she loved herself. So she got into the van with her dog, skinny as a greyhound from chasing crabs and seafoam, and left behind that happy wooden house without knowing it would be forever; that her grandmother would fall down dead in the fields a few months later, between the rows of corn; and that her father, out of grief, guilt, and necessity, would hastily sell off the house, land, and animals.

The pain over the death of her grandmother didn't drive Mom insane because she was in love with a boy, and that boy was everything Mom ever dreamed of. She fantasized obsessively about the day that he would save her from that house, from her mother's beatings, from her brothers who stole everything from her, inviting over all their friends who had suddenly turned into gawking men. She sobbed over her grandmother day and night but all that crying made her face and eyes swell, and the boy told her that she looked ugly like that and that he liked to see her looking pretty. So she pushed all the pain down into her stomach, malformed, like a little dead fetus.

A month later, Mom was riding around in her boyfriend's sports car. After dancing to slow songs all night, the boy drove Mom home and before leaving he asked her for a kiss. Mom said no, not because she was chaste, but out of fear that her mother would beat her to death. The boy sped off, making his tires squeal and his engine roar.

Before leaving, he called her a prude, cruel, inhuman.

Later that night Mom heard a whistle under her window: her boyfriend's whistle. She wanted to play hard to get, to make him pay for his rudeness, but the boy whistled and whistled, and Mom heard the sounds of a guitar and the boy serenading her with love songs, saying, "I adore you, you are my whole world." She got up, pushed back the curtains, and leaned out the window to shout that she loved him too, but there was no one there.

That's what Mom said, and then she went quiet, pensive. After a little while she said again that there was no one there.

"I looked out the window and there was no one there."

She remembered her grandmother's warning and she waited all the next day, petrified with fear, for someone to come take her, for terrible things to happen, for something. But nothing out of the ordinary happened: she went to school, her mom slapped her for getting home late, a friend taught her how to put on eyeliner, her father found all his shirts and nice pants had been tossed out onto the street and he cried silently, her brothers told her that if they ever found out she'd slept with someone they'd kill her, she made a chocolate cake to sell at the fair.

After a few days, Mom, dressed up like a soldier, met a man from the city at a parade, and she felt that when he spoke to her—she said—it was like a multicolored hummingbird had flown into her mouth.

Mom broke up with her sports-car-driving boyfriend that very night, and a year later, she and Dad were married in an epic wedding where they ate all the shrimp in the world, then bought kitchen appliances, moved to the city, had a little girl, went on vacation to the beach, watched their faces deform until they were unrecognizable to themselves, learned the hidden codes in each other's silences, called each other by made-up names and coded sounds—Dad three little high-pitched whistles, Mom a hummed note—they loved each other, they hated each other, they loved each other again, they got old, and one day they saved a little puppy from abandonment only to have it die poisoned a few hours later.

Dad stopped loving Mom when I was about fifteen. We could smell the cheap liquor on his breath despite the hard candies he sucked on, we found a hand mirror and fuchsia lipstick in the car's glove compartment, a woman called at midnight on New Year's and he said it was a friend but Dad didn't have any friends, much less any female friends.

Mom knew, of course she knew, but she never opened her mouth. She shoved her voice back into the darkness of her throat, like someone taken hostage by terrorists. They went out to do the shopping, attended events, he spoke and she answered, and Mom once again let her urge to cry and scream fester in her belly like a little malformed baby. The entire house was filled with toxic fumes, like a garbage dump. Dad sucked up all the available oxygen and we gasped for breaths of the deadly gases that clung to the walls and lingered in the corners.

Why don't you shout at him, Mom? Why don't you tell him to go to hell? Why don't you poison his food? Why don't you cut his clothes up with garden shears? Why don't you tell him you want a divorce, Mom? Why don't you stop blending in with the sofa, the curtains, the wallpaper, you stupid chameleon, why don't you step forward from wherever you're hiding and force him to look you in the face? Why don't you scream like a madwoman, Mom?

I never asked those questions. They stayed together.

Mom put up with it and put up with it, even took care of Dad when cancer left him a sad little weakling who couldn't get up to go to the bathroom but could still send messages to the other woman and, who knows, maybe even to another son, another daughter. She took care of Dad when his breathing was reduced to a long, slow high-pitched whistle that pierced her eardrums. She took care of him to the last day and cried at his funeral. I didn't ask the questions that would make Mom ashamed of her whole life, embarrassed for giving him the right side of the bed and the best cuts of turkey—thin slices of light meat. I didn't want to point out how in exchange she'd destroyed her own self-love and become a miserable prisoner, living in futile silence for fear that he would leave her, like a hand over her nose and mouth, suffocating her. The only sound a whistle.

CHOSEN

Thy dead men shall live,
together with my dead body shall they arise.
Awake and sing, ye that dwell in dust:
for thy dew is as the dew of herbs,
and the earth shall cast out the dead.
                                                    —ISAIAH 26:19

On the road to Mar Bravo there's a cemetery for poor people. It became a pilgrimage site for the chosen ones because four of their own were buried there. Between the graves adorned with artificial flowers faded by the sun, headstones with chipped corners, and weeds, the girls cried with their sparkling skin, their white blouses, their jean shorts, their beaded necklaces, and their strappy sandals. They hugged and patted one another like nymphs before the body of a lamb. Beside them, with dry eyes and their hands clenched in fists by their sides, stood the males of the species: boys with hair falling into their eyes, their arms deliciously hard. Freckled, smooth-skinned, silent, and sullen like geniuses or like idiots, so handsome it was scary.

Among the carpenters, seamstresses, fishermen, and babies malnourished from the womb, they buried the four surfers from Punta Carnero. The parents had decided that their sons should be laid to rest in that gray cemetery and not in the rich people's one, with a lawn as green as a parrot, fresh roses—red and shameless, brought in by refrigerated truck—and marble headstones with religious inscriptions below the long surnames. They thought that the corpses of the most beautiful drowned men in the world should remain forever beside the sea. There were four of them; they would inherit the earth. The night before their deaths they'd broken a combined total of seventy-seven hearts at the yacht club party, kissing their gorgeous girlfriends and grabbing their little asses through their sundresses. At dawn, still drunk, they sheathed themselves in black neoprene and, only their skulls exposed, went out to brave the rough waves, convinced of their boy-god immortality. The sea spit them out on the seventh day, soft and whitish like newborns.

We always drank there, outside the Mar Bravo cemetery, because what else did we have to do? All the parties were private, by invitation only. Beautiful boys invited beautiful girls, average boys invited beautiful girls, hideous boys invited beautiful girls. Doors that looked like the gates of heaven opened up for other girls—but never for us. One time we tried to get into a party and the bouncer told us that it was for friends only and we answered: "Whose friends?" But the man was already lifting his pretenses of security, the velvet rope the color of blood, for an athletic, angular, smiling girl who looked like someone out of tampon commercial. We were dying to find out what went on behind those pearly gates, even though we instinctively knew that there was no place for us there, that once inside our defects would multiply until we choked on them, that we'd become a hyperbole of ourselves, fun-house mirror versions: the fat one, the butch one, the lanky one, the flat one, the hunchback. Just as the pretty girls would become even more attractive together, their collective virtues masking any individual defects to make one another look better until they shone like one giant star, girls like us are an obscene spectacle when assembled, our failings exacerbated into a kind of freak show: we become even more monstrous.

We knew, of course we knew, that not even the most desperate boys, not even those who were overweight, nerdy, or goth, would approach us. The only people who approach girls like us are girls like us. Why even bother? We were free to go anywhere we wanted, and we hated that: We longed for the beautiful girls' lack of freedom, for the arms of our boyfriends like yokes around our necks, for quickies in the pool house without a condom, for big baseball-player handprints on our asses. We wanted to be taken by force and with every thrust to squeal the beautiful names of those beautiful boys. We wanted to spread our legs for them and grab their perfect hair when we came, knots the color of sand between our fingers. We wanted to make sweet cocktails and witches' brews from the nectar of their sexes. We wanted the pretty girls to disappear, to slice off their heads with flaming machetes. We wanted to enter those private parties mounted on flying nags to bursts of thunder and shouting and lightning and earthquakes and to rain down on those beautiful idiots a plague of locusts and serpents. We wanted to make the pretty girls kneel before us, powerful Amazon warriors that we were, and for them to watch helplessly as their men climbed, enchanted and docile, onto the backs of our horses. We wanted, we wanted, we wanted. We were pure want.

And pure rage.

The day will come, yes sir, when everyone will notice us and will say to anyone who will listen: Love them. Love them. And that mandate will travel the earth. The day will come when we wipe away each and every one of our tears.

In the meantime, we had a car, we had money, we had the night, and we had nothing.

We would park outside the cemetery with plenty of alcohol, plenty of weed, plenty of pills, and plenty of cigarettes. At least we had that, the means to get fucked up, to sully our bodies with something perverse, to feel like bad girls. Virgins, incredibly obscene. Morbid, lonely. How great it would've felt to be desired by one another: to desire our friendly tongues, to reach ecstasy with only our fingers inside each other, to find the tender, juicy flesh and flower between our legs. Being a lover is so different from being a loser. To throw a passing glance at the closed doors of the private parties and feel thankful not to be there, bored, with some idiot's stiff, wet tongue in our ears or leaving horrible marks on our necks. We should've found love among ourselves, but we are who we are and what we are is almost always cruel.

It was dark except for the light of the car. Few people drove the road to Mar Bravo except maybe some couple looking to fuck on the overlook, maybe someone looking to commit suicide. The night was ripe for sexual rituals, death, and resurrection. The moon dripped red upon the world like a deflowered youth, and the radio played songs of men in love and women we would never be. The cemetery under that moon looked like it was about to break into a boil. We each put a pill on another's tongue and we passed the bottle around until it was almost empty. Suddenly we thought about the drowned boys at Punta Carnero and their beauty that transcended life and surely transcended death. We thought about those adored, delicious boys, their impossible parties and impossible waves, now sleeping beneath us. We got out of the car and filed into the cemetery to dance in the light of the blood moon, shaking our thin dresses and our night-time hair. We danced like we'd never danced, as if we'd always danced, as if we'd arrived at the party celebrating the end of the world and the bouncer, upon seeing us, had lifted the plush velvet rope with a deep bow. We danced like brides on our wedding nights, and as if in some sexual delirium, we ripped the clothes from one another's bodies until we were naked before the silence of the dead. We danced waving our dresses like garlands of flowers and we kissed on the lips and we touched one another's firm breasts, howling with pleasure. We sang hymns of vengeance with muffled trumpets as our imaginary background music. We were angels pouring justice onto our bodies and into our desires, opening ourselves up in chorus with the night-blooming flowers, exuding the same smell of musk and sea. We searched for our boys among the dead and discovered that someone had gotten there first. From the half-opened coffins fell hands gleaming like porcelain in the moonlight. They were still wearing their clothes, black and navy suits that had slow-danced with beautiful girls in pastel dresses. Their shoes had been taken, as well as their watches, chains, rings, and everything that could be bitten to know if it was valuable, but they'd left the little silk pocket squares in their suit jackets, handkerchiefs to dry all of our tears.

We asked them to dance and they said yes and they danced with us, timid and distant at first, then ever closer, with their cold faces pressed to our warm necks. They said, we're sure they said, that they preferred being there with us to anywhere else, that they preferred us to the little princesses of their kingdoms. After dancing we sat on their graves, each of us with a perfect boy whispering his dreams to us, giggling like idiots, asking for kisses through fluttered lashes. The kisses came and the madness followed, desire crashing like violent waves against our backs. The dawn found us naked, mounted atop the erect sexes of our lovers, galloping like ferocious jockeys, plunging headlong into the world, ready to destroy it.

SISTER

We met Mariela when we were fourteen. She showed up at school out of nowhere looking like some Sherpa: carrying a huge, filthy backpack loaded with who knows what while the rest of us girls had only a notebook and a pencil case filled with brand-new pens and beautiful pencils, super sharp. We all noticed her, pasty, skinny, hunched over like a question mark, with a uniform that was too small in the chest and socks so tiny it looked like she wasn't wearing any. Maybe she wasn't wearing any. She also wasn't wearing a slip, which was mandatory, and we could see her pink panties through her skirt: *The nuns are going to chew her up the very first day, what a mess, where was the girl's mother when she left the house?*

If it had been halfway through the year, Mariela might not have looked so much like a turd, but it was the first day of school—the rest of us were flawless, our hair straightened, everything so new it squeaked, and she, to be honest, didn't smell great.

Your destiny is set from day one and Mariela was immediately marked as an outsider even by the outsiders. Pure periphery.

During break she stood at one end of the volleyball court and waited for some other girls to come play. No one went near her. So she just bounced the ball alone until the bell rang and didn't seem the slightest bit bothered. Like a dog who, not encountering any other dogs, is perfectly content to play with a stick.

My cousin met her on the school bus. Mariela was like a little girl: clumsy, excited, submissive. She wore her greasy hair sectioned off with a bunch of colorful barrettes, she laughed with her mouth wide open, showing all her tiny teeth with dark tips, and when she squinted her eyes—she was shortsighted but didn't wear glasses—she looked like an abused puppy.

My cousin didn't have friends so much as followers, and Mariela was a perfect candidate because everything seemed to indicate she had a total lack of will, bordering on zombie. And she had money in her pocket. And a pool. And, most of all, she seemed oblivious to the fact that my cousin was using her, that she didn't even really like her.

They quickly became inseparable and I, whom my cousin treated like some accessory she could put on and take off at her convenience, only halfway made it into the friendship. My cousin's form of caring was anything but disinterested: I was born to be her inferior, her minion. Our family had branded me thusly and so she treated me accordingly.

Some people are born to incite their loved ones' baser instincts, their desire to subjugate others, their perversity.

Around the dinner table, like deranged generals before a map of hostile lands, the adults corralled, attacked, and destroyed us. They decided that I—dark, squat, coarse, chubby—was enemy territory, a stain on the bloodline, the product of the shameful things our ancestors did to the dark-skinned natives. My cousin, on the other hand, was of a cleaner race, superior, the image that they wanted people to conjure when they uttered our last name aloud.

Predetermination, it's called.

Mariela was a ventriloquist's dummy: *I'm not the one laughing at you, cuz, it's Mariela.*

But it was worse to stay at home and have my parents pity me for being a loser, Mom coming into my room to give me the most nauseating smile: a smile that said what a shame you're so fat, I feel sorry for you, everything you're missing, the best life has to offer, boys' burning gazes, being wanted, being pretty, and then Dad would start the classic fight about you're doing a terrible job with her, look how huge she is, make her exercise, do something, she's your daughter.

When we were little girls, my cousin and I wore the same size and ate the same food. We both loved condensed milk, pink slushies, fresh bread, gummies, rice with corn. As we grew up I still liked all that stuff, but she stopped. With the food went her good nature, her humor, the person she was before she became obsessed with mirrors. I imagine being hungry all the time would make you heartless. People congratulated her for it—our grandma practically broke into a round of applause every time she saw her. Maybe it's not so bad to have your spark of life snuffed out in exchange for being skinny.

Every night I prayed to be snuffed out like her, to be skinny like her, to transform into her, but the next day, with the first grumble of my stomach, I knew that god had performed no miracle. I hated the god that created me in his image and likeness: I hated myself.

Quickly, over a matter of months, we stopped being us. As our clothes size grew more distant—from eight to six to four for her, ten, twelve, fourteen for me—another insurmountable distance grew. She moved over to the side of the winners and no matter how hard I stretched my chubby fingers, I could never again touch her.

I was left alone. A lonely fat girl.

The rift between us, which our grandma scratched at with the hard nail of her index finger, deepened, became extremely painful, raw: she was skinny and I wasn't, she was popular and I wasn't, she was loved and I wasn't.

"Your cousin is such a striking young lady, don't you agree?"

My cousin's worst fear was fatness, her own fatness. Sometimes she ate hardly anything and sometimes she ate a whole, whole, whole lot and then vomited it up. She would disappear into the bathroom for an hour after every meal and I would hear her make that horrible sound like when you want to expel from your body something that your body does not want to let go of. Exorcism, she called it.

"Be right back, I'm going to give myself an exorcism."

It was torture when my aunt and uncle forced her to sit at the table with us. Someone told her that you had to chew each bite a hundred times to keep from getting fat. All of us would be sitting there with empty plates and she'd only be on her third or fourth mouthful. I once caught her slipping those little chewed-up bites into the pockets of her school-uniform skirt when no one was looking.

One unbearably hot afternoon I was lying on her bed watching TV and she, like always, was jumping around, doing aerobics or dancing. Suddenly I saw her pick up the scissors she always had around because she liked to cut actresses and models out of magazines and stick them to the mirror, windows, and walls. She told me that at night the models' eyes turned red and they shouted at her in terrifying voices, calling her *piggy, piggy, piggy*. I asked her why she didn't take them down. She told me because they called her *piggy, piggy, piggy*.

She placed the scissors against the inside of her thighs. I watched, terrified. She grabbed a piece of flesh in her hand and put the scissors in the middle of it. She told me that nothing would make her happier than to cut off that fatness. Then she started punching her legs and her stomach, crying, begging god to make her skinny.

"I hate it, I hate it, I hate it, I hate it."

I told her that I loved her, that I loved every part of her, that ever since we were little girls she'd been everything to me, the most beautiful, and she responded that my love didn't do her any good.

When Mariela came into our lives my cousin was a skinny teenager that the family considered genetic perfection and the one that all the boys were in love with. I, on the other hand, was a booger that clung to her like something deathly, the buffoon, a dark, ugly cloud who only served to make her light shine brighter by comparison. She was the sun of our surname, the only part of the family crest that mattered.

My grandmother made it perfectly clear one day when I asked what they were going to give me for Christmas.

"Until you lose some weight, we're going to give all your presents to your cousin."

This wasn't strictly true. If only it had been. She got the Crystal Barbie I'd been dreaming about, and they gave me Pregnant Barbie. She whispered in my ear that I had the same belly as my doll. I told my mom and she burst out laughing.

There's an age at which you either lose yourself or you win yourself.

My cousin won herself. They let me lose myself.

Mariela's house was in a neighborhood that had fallen out of fashion. Rich people move in herds, like goats, all together, and the once-desirable addresses, the white, solemn mansions, had been taken over by technological institutes, evangelical churches, and ghosts. In that area the wetlands licked at the patios. The snakes, iguanas, rats, and insects wandered the streets at all hours, like they owned them.

The house was huge, really huge. My entire block could've fit in their living room. It had a dining room that was equally gigantic and a marble staircase that seemed to spill down from the top floor. The living room had immense windows that looked out onto a terrace from which you could walk down to the yard, the pool, and way at the back, the wetlands, like an eye watching all of us.

Unlike all the other houses we'd been to, at Mariela's you immediately sensed, understood, that you could do absolutely anything you wanted.

It reeked of abandonment, the same smell Mariela gave off, the stench of a beggar. The plants lived or died without anyone's interference: they turned yellow if it didn't rain and green if it did. There were dirty clothes, socks, and shoes everywhere. The fine furniture was scratched and dirty, the armchairs were missing their cushions and faded by our relentless sun, the sofa had been sliced down the middle as if an autopsy had been performed on it.

Every time we visited there seemed to be fewer paintings on the walls, fewer vases, fewer mirrors, less elegance: like they'd moved in backward. Mariela said that those things were expensive and people would always pay good money for them. We didn't know whether to believe her, but the truth was that the place looked like a mansion whose owners, after going bankrupt, had fled the country.

The silence was incredible. Everything felt far away, spongy, unreal. Sometimes we drifted away from one another like the islands we were: three children on their own, learning to be women without anyone's guidance.

Lying around the pool, where the lawn had turned to weeds, we sunk down until we'd almost disappeared and fantasized about boys, music, clothes, makeup, while inside other desires and other fears grew like algae, like mold, like claws, like STDs, like poison gases.

Love, for example, loving and being loved, loomed over us as we talked about other things, and our little girls' voices became the voices of women who lied.

As we copied the choreography of the coolest new music video, as we danced around imitating our favorite artists, inside us the tides were turning, swelling, frightening away the birds, terrifying our guardian angels, making us sick.

The age of innocence is the age of violence.

One of those afternoons my cousin and I were

complaining about our parents, about their willful blindness, their aggressions disguised as concern, their violent way of turning their backs on us as we, teenage girls, that other type of newborn, cried and cried in every way possible for a shred of consolation.

Mariela, who never talked about her family even though we asked her all the time, said that her parents would've preferred for her to be the dead one. We didn't know how to respond. The three of us sat staring at the sky, sinking into the bog, alone and rotting like corpses.

Fat girls live on lies. Starving girls live on helplessness. Lonely girls live on pain. Girls always, always, always feed off the abyss.

"Do you have any siblings, Mariela?"

"No. I once dreamed I had a little sister: she was adorable, tiny, and my parents were crazy about her. They stopped paying attention to me. In the dream I thought that if I drowned her in the pool, they'd love me again. Then I woke up."

She shrugged her shoulders and dove into the water.

The pool was filthy, greenish milk, a swamp. I did what I could so that we could swim without being afraid. I used the net to fish out crickets, bats, water roaches, flowers, branches, the odd iguana, and even drowned rats, but the green algae on the bottom, dense as suede, was impossible to get rid of. We tried to keep from touching it so that it wouldn't mix with the water. I sometimes went under and with the tip of my toe I would brush that velvety surface, and I was disgusted but it also felt good: the water was immediately muddied and it looked like you were floating in something that wasn't water, more like amniotic fluid, formaldehyde, gastric acid.

The tropics degrade, debase.

I didn't like taking my clothes off because the two of them, Mariela and my cousin, were skinny and I wasn't, and I knew they looked at my fat rolls and my thunder thighs, comparing them to Mariela's flat stomach and my cousin's long legs, but once I got in the pool there was no getting me out: in the water I was a mermaid and I didn't care that my cousin thought of me as her pet or that Ricardo, the boy I loved, was secretly in love with her and not me.

Sometimes they would wrap up in towels and go back inside, and I would stay by myself in the pool, doing somersaults, dancing, fantasizing about being so weightless in real life. Sometimes it turned to night and I would remain submerged, caressed by the algae in the darkness, in that blackening water more and more like the sea. Sometimes I felt a hand gripping my ankle and I thought, *Take me with you, thing of the water, take me to wherever it is you live.*

One day when the boys were over, my cousin suggested we play a game where you spin a bottle and the person has to answer your question. She knew I had such a huge crush on Ricardo that it left me breathless, that I wrote poems to him in my notebooks during every class and I dedicated love songs to him on the radio without leaving my name.

A fat girl's passions are comical, like when a tiny dog tries to mount a gigantic one, like when a monkey loves.

Several times the bottle landed so that my cousin

could ask Ricardo a question, and every time she asked him the same thing:

"Do you like my cousin?"

"Why not?"

"Why not?"

"Why not?"

First he answered no, then he answered because no, then because he just didn't like me, then because he liked someone else, then because he wanted to hook up with the other girl, then, fed up, that because I was super fat and he didn't like fat girls and why didn't someone take my food away from me, and, finally, that because he liked her and he was in love with her.

There are moments in every life in which understanding happens at a deeper level, beyond a person's capacity to comprehend. Your bones understand, your fat understands, your half-digested hamburger understands, your pancreas understands, your bile understands, your snot, your membranes, your hair, your nails, every drop of your blood understands. I understood that there were feelings like infections: capable of making your body rot with gangrene in a matter of seconds, like a grotesque mouth devouring you, bathing your insides in mercury, crashing into you like a cannonball. If I had dropped dead right then and there, I would've done so knowing that existence is pure horror, being alive is pure horror.

And once you know that, you can't unknow it.

The night my cousin and Ricardo fell in love I dreamed that I saw her floating facedown in Mariela's pool. I wasn't scared.

One Friday we slept over and the electricity went out.

The house was perfect in a blackout because it was almost completely empty and the palm trees cast incredible shadows, like giants wearing headdresses, on the naked walls. Also, you could put candles everywhere without any mom complaining that the wax would stain the wood or ruin the tablecloth.

That night my cousin told us all about Ricardo's lips, Ricardo's tongue, Ricardo's hands, and I remembered that dream. It was the first of many times to come over the following years that I would think about killing myself. It was the first time, also, that I thought about killing.

How easily a candle consumes everything it touches with its hungry tongue. How easy to set fire to fabric, plastic, two-toned school-uniform shoes, long, light hair like my cousin's.

Fire consumes flesh and does not regurgitate it.

My cousin said she was bored and suggested we play Ouija. For the first time since meeting her, Mariela said no. My cousin gave her a look that was like twisting her arm.

"Why not, Mariela?"

"Because no."

My cousin, of course, paid as little mind to Mariela as to a fruit fly and proceeded to take out a piece of paper and draw the sun, the moon, the alphabet, a yes, a no, a hello, and a goodbye.

Mariela left the living room, but we could hear her. She let out a sound that was either a cry or a moan or a prayer or an invocation. It was an unexpected sound, accustomed as we were to her constant idiotic laugh, her shrill, off-key singing, her little squeal when someone pushed her in the water. I was surprised that Mariela was capable of crying or doing whatever she was doing, of doing anything besides laughing.

My cousin wasn't a person who'd console someone she considered inferior, so she continued drawing the Ouija board as I, leaning against the wall, thought of death, my own death, my cousin's, death to that house and that city.

Mariela returned. Even in the dark I could see the change in her: she lumbered in heavily, like a monster in a black-and-white movie. She stared silently at the ground and in her face there was a stiffness, like an old lady, like a widow, like a drug addict.

At first I thought that Mariela, like me, had finally realized her place in the world: a dog kennel lent to her by people like my cousin on the condition that she smiled and thanked them for it. I thought Mariela's way of walking, that slowness, that heaviness, came from an understanding that from her position, stripped of all dignity, it wasn't possible to say no. Even if we're scared, even if it suffocates us, even if our insides blaze with shame, even if it makes us hate ourselves: we underlings must serve up our heads on a platter so the pretty ones can rummage around in our eyes, nostrils, and mouth, and say, *How disgusting.*

But Mariela looked at us differently, as if from above. That new Mariela, with a depraved look in her eyes and her black-toothed smile, decided to humor my cousin, who insisted we use the Ouija board like she didn't know what always happens when wounded teenagers use Ouija boards.

We sat in a circle of candles. My cousin was buzzing

with triumph and superiority, feeling not only beautiful but reckless. She looked at us with her nostrils flared: the poor idiot and the poor obese girl, I'm better than both of you.

She began to move an upside-down glass across the page, calling the names of dead actors and singers, but nothing happened. Minutes went by; nothing happened.

Suddenly a gust of wind that sounded like a howling dog blew out the candles and we were thrown into darkness. My cousin screamed. The glass had moved on its own.

"Is there someone there?"

The three of us heard it. The glass slid violently across the page.

I relit the candles and saw that my cousin was crying. Pale and panicked, she reached out to rip up the piece of paper. I said no, that we had to dismiss the spirit first, that if we didn't it would stay at Mariela's house forever.

My cousin looked toward the pool, terrified, as if she expected some corpse to come walking toward her with its arms outstretched, eyeless, black water running down its legs.

Our fingers on the glass, we began asking the spirit questions: Its name. Its age. How it died. The glass moved wildly, desperately. It slid off the page and then came back.

Mariela spoke for the first time since we'd started playing.

"She doesn't know how to write."

The glass darted around erratically no matter what we asked. My cousin was shaking and crying. Someone had pulled her hair. Someone, something, had bit her cheek. We heard, first very far away and then almost in our ears, the laughter of a small child. All the doors, even the sliding ones, closed with a bang. A pink ball bounced down the marble stairs. The glass flew through the air and shattered against the wall. The palm trees started shaking like enormous pregnant witches dancing in the night.

Mariela stood up and slapped my cousin across the face, and it sounded like thunder in the darkness.

"Idiot, you woke her up."

Mariela's voice sounded beastly, like the roar of some malignant creature, like when a storm makes landfall. My cousin asked, in a whisper, who she'd woken up. Despite the terror, a part of me enjoyed the mousy voice of absolute submission that escaped my cousin's little pink mouth.

"Who, Marielita?"

The lights came back on with a flash. The house seemed to make a sound of surprise and the appliances began to pant. Mariela stood up. "Come," she said. "Come with me."

We didn't want to go, but we didn't want to stay there by ourselves either. We followed Mariela up the stairs and down a long hallway. The geometric-patterned carpeting ended in a door with a name in pink letters surrounded by little animals: *Lucía*.

My cousin, once again in the voice of a little mouse, asked, "Marielita, who is Lucía?"

"You're about to find out."

She opened the door and the first thing we noticed was the freezing cold. A lamp spinning in circles projected little shadows of elephants, lions, and monkeys onto the ceiling and walls. It played a lullaby. In the center of the room was a crib draped in yellowed lace beside a bed where two people slept covered in blankets.

It smelled strange. Despite the fact that it was freezing, a smell of rot, gaseous and sweet, reached our noses and flooded our heads, our brains. My cousin started crying and once again Mariela slapped her.

"My parents hate crying, that's why I never cry."

I stood in the doorway as Mariela grabbed my cousin by the hand and dragged her to the edge of the little crib. "She wants to see you," she told her. "She wants you to hold her. She's chosen you."

My cousin bent down and pulled away several baby blankets like shrouds.

Then she let out a beastly wail. Frantic, eyes bulging, she tried to run away but Mariela gripped her arm. My cousin kept screaming and screaming until Mariela hit her so hard that blood began to pour from her nose.

The couple sat up in bed, first the woman and then the man. The woman asked what was going on. Mariela answered that her little sister was hungry, very hungry, but that she was about to feed her. The lamp kept turning, projecting little jungle animals onto my cousin's horrified face, her mouth open inhumanly wide, her eyes filled with terror.

"I'll take care of it, Mommy. Don't worry."

LORENA

For Lorena Gallo

Angelita tells me that she's going to introduce me to the man of my dreams and I say, "Again?" She says, "Yes, yes, he's cute and perfect for you." I put on cat-eye eyeliner and sparkly lipstick because I'm sure to at least get some kisses out of this. The guy is a gringo and I like gringos. Yes. I like that they smell like Dial soap and laundry detergent and nothing else. I like how they have those perfect white teeth. I like that they are sort of dopey. I like that they pay for everything without thinking twice. I like that they are so childlike and grateful in bed, how they say oh god oh god, and how they come with cum that doesn't smell like anything, or maybe a little like Dial, like Tide. I'm going to fuck the gringo. I put on a tight, low-cut top and underwear I bought out of a catalog that lifts my flat butt into a spectacular, amazing ass.

We go to a Mexican place because the gringos, no matter what they say, think we're all Mexican and that we'll feel at home there and that Mexican food makes us horny. Yeah, sexy mama. After three huge pitchers of margaritas we start to dance, and the gringo, who isn't all shy like I imagined he'd be and looks like he's super kinky with those devilish green eyes, slips his hands inside my underwear and slides his finger between my ass cheeks. Oh, this gringo. I love it. He looks like a prince out of a fairy tale: brown hair, white skin, tall and muscular. And to top it off, he's aggressive. If I hadn't moved his hands, he'd have stripped me naked right in front of all these people who are already scandalized by us, and there's a Mexican lady making the sign of the cross. We don't even make it home. We fuck as soon as we get in the car. He's a whirlwind of virility, size, girth, skill. Oh, this gringo. He's still a gringo, he still says, "Yes, yes, yes," all yeses and all "Oh god," and we both come until we almost pass out from pleasure. Drunk from fucking, we look at each other and burst out laughing. Like a couple of idiots. Maybe this guy really is the man of my dreams like Angelita said.

We keep going at his house. We fuck like animals, nonstop, shrieking, all night Saturday and into Sunday morning. He penetrates me and eats me and drinks me and swallows me and impales me and licks me and pummels me until I pass out from pleasure. When I get home Sunday night, I look in the mirror: my lips are swollen, my nipples bitten, almost purple, and my neck is covered in hickeys. I smile like a teenager. I'm in love with the gringo sex god. But it's just sex, Lore, he's not even going to call. I can barely walk and my vagina burns: I get in bed and pass out from exhaustion. Monday after work I talk to Angelita on the phone. She laughs and squeals with embarrassment. "Slut!" she says to me. "You're such a slut, Lore." Her roommate kicks her out for being too noisy and she tells me that John asked her about me, that he wants to ask me out again, that he likes me a lot. Now

I'm the one squealing. Loudly, like a madwoman, until the neighbors bang on the walls and threaten to call the cops. Chill out, motherfuckers, leave me alone.

John and I are married in front of a few friends. His family is not very accepting of him marrying a Latina they hardly know, a manicurist, an immigrant, my god, but he doesn't give a damn. I wear pink flowers in my hair and he wears his blue military uniform. I love him so much when I see him there at the altar, waiting for me, so gringo, so tall, so handsome. My heart jumps in my chest. A girl like me, selling makeup door to door, doing rich ladies' nails, never imagines that her dreams could come true.

A girl like me always expects the worst.

John turns me on like nobody in the world. A hunger that feeds on hunger. Our sex life is our entire life, we don't care about anyone or anything else: we stop watching TV, going out, seeing people. We spend all our time fucking. Never has a man made me feel the way my gringo does, my John, what an animal, my American dream with a cock.

I don't know if this happens to all women, but after fucking I feel like our love is a living thing, like I could stretch out my hands and touch it and hug it tight like it's a helium balloon and float away. Sometimes I imagine that I see the two of us from above, sweaty and shiny from all the sex, and I love the image of my body next to his.

Us, Lorena and John, John and Lorena, a single entity.

We can never run out of Budweiser. It's like they're sponsoring us. If we run out for any reason John loses his mind. His face turns red and he blames me: You never think of me. He grabs the car keys and goes out to buy a few twelve-packs. When there's football on, he can down twenty cans without coming up for air.

A woman doesn't just wake up one morning knowing that that's the day her life is going to go to shit. Day one of so many to follow. If we at least knew, if it were outlined in red like the saints' days on the calendar, we could prepare for it, stay away from it, protect ourselves. The days follow the nights and, as that dance as old as time continues on, darkness slips into the house.

I'm washing the dishes. He's drinking. I tell him to slow down a little, that he's had like ten beers in an hour. He stands up from the couch, he throws me against the wall, and he spits at me. He says I'm a stupid fucking Latina and that a stupid fucking Latina isn't going to tell him how much beer he can drink. Then he shakes up one of the cans, opens it, and sprays it all over the kitchen that I just cleaned. Foam covers me, coats the spotless dishes, the gleaming knives, the pots and pans throwing off the reflection of his rage and my fear.

Like an evil spirit that haunts the house, stalking you from the bathroom to the bedroom and then to the dining room, the man who isn't the man I love floats around like a ghost, a demon. He never leaves.

Every time I speak he mimics me, and the voice he uses is the voice of a person with mental problems. "That's how you talk," he laughs, "you talk like a moron." I tell him to try speaking another language, being a foreigner. He slaps me so hard my head swivels, he puts his huge hand around my throat, he says he's never going to be a foreigner because we foreigners are all losers and that if I talk back again he's going to beat me until I have to be put in a wheelchair.

I stop talking. Every time I have to say something to him I practice it ten times in my head and when it comes out of my mouth it sounds like the canned voice of a language teacher. He laughs even harder. "You embarrass me," he says, "you're like a trained animal, you're ugly, hideous, why did I marry you." If it weren't for him, he tells me, I'd be on the corner like all the other Latina whores in this country. "I'm going to have you deported, you're nothing, you're trash."

The man who says these things to me in the living room comes to sleep in my bed at night. With ten or twenty beers in him, all he wants to do is hurt me. A woman who swore she loved a man before his friends and the eyes of god shouldn't have to scrub the bloodstains off their marriage bed after her husband rips her open. A woman in love shouldn't have to disinfect intimate wounds. A woman shouldn't have to cry in fear every time her husband comes to bed.

He's always so drunk.

When I get home from work I find him on the couch surrounded by empty beer cans. His beautiful gringo face has transformed: he still has his green eyes, but they look deranged, a face that would leave you terrified if you encountered it in a dark alley. The dark alley is my kitchen, and the attacker wears a ring with my name engraved inside it.

I don't say a word to anyone. I don't want them to hate John, I don't want them to pity me, I don't want to get divorced because they've always told me that a woman who gets divorced is a sinner. I also don't want my family to find out I'm one of those women we've all heard about so many times—who puts up with the beatings from my violent, alcoholic husband because even if he hits me, even if he kills me, he's still my husband, saying *I fell* from behind sunglasses, repeating over and over, even when no one asks, *My husband is under a lot of pressure.*

No bride, in her ruffled dress with flowers in her hair, imagines she'll become one of those women everyone talks about, the other ladies closing their eyes and shaking their heads when her name comes up, one of those women who can be described using words like battered, raped, abused, murdered.

No bride imagines she'll be anything except happy.

John hits me in public. We're leaving the supermarket with our groceries and we pass a man. He goes crazy, says I was flirting with him, how is it possible I'm such a slut, that I deserve to be killed, that he fantasizes about shooting me in the stomach and watching me fall down in slow motion, ripping out my heart while I'm still alive and showing it to me and eating it. The other people in the parking lot see him and hear him. The words *whore*, *piggy*, *disgusting*, *dirty* fly through the air like poison darts. He, a huge man, punches me in the face and pushes me to the ground. No one comes over to help, no one says anything. "Get in the car or I'll run you over, slut," he says.

There's football on almost every night in the summer. He's drunk, like always, stumbling and tripping over everything as he comes into the bedroom. He gets naked and in the dim light I can see his erection, that cock I once adored, that I caressed as if it were the face of my baby, that I put in my mouth and sucked to draw nourishment from. It's been a long time since I've wanted him inside me, to cradle him in my skin and envelop him in my wetness until we both explode with pleasure. Every time he rapes me I remember the amazing feeling of our first encounters, the hot ring of my vagina, my clit like a beating heart and all that hot molasses that he'd lick and lick until he left me clean as a newborn babe. Once we were beautiful—now we're soaked in blood.

He lifts the sheets and rips off my underwear. I say, "No, not again, no." I say, "Please, John," and he shoves himself inside me like an electric drill. I don't know how long it lasts, but the pain rips my flesh open as if I were being penetrated with fire. I leave my body and float above the two people on the bed below, woman and man, wife and husband, raped and rapist, and I think I shouldn't be seeing this, that no one should see this.

He falls asleep. Bloody, his cum dripping between my legs, I get up. I walk to the kitchen and in the darkness I see it, shining like the star of Bethlehem, showing me the way. I grab it firmly by the handle and return to the bedroom.

LEECHES

Julito's mom treated him not like a boy but like a god. The other moms would watch us cry, glance at our skinned knees, send us to wash the scrape with soap, then hit us for fighting—"Little snot-nosed brats"—but Julito's mom would jump up in a state of panic—"My son, my beautiful boy"—she'd treat his scratch as if it were an amputation, give him a cookie, kiss the wound, and sing to him "Sana sana colita de rana." The other ladies would say, "Ay, María Teresa, it's no big deal, kids are made of rubber." She would respond that Julito wasn't made of rubber: he was made of chocolate, of sugar, honey, angels' wings.

They would laugh with tipsiness after having drunk several bottles of Julito's mom's good wine.

Since my mom was the only one who drove, she would give the other moms a ride back to their houses at the end of the afternoon, and on the way they would talk about Julito's mom.

"It's shameful, the way she's spoiling that little boy."

"Well, it's understandable, she's an older mother. I was convinced María Teresa would be alone forever, then one day she turned up pregnant. God forgive me, but if I'd known my child was going to turn out like that, I would've gotten rid of it."

"I would've kept him. You have to take the child god sends you."

"God had nothing to do with it! It was the other one who sent the boy."

"You're terrible!"

"But listen, she keeps that boy neat as a pin. She must spend a fortune on clothes; I never see the little monster wear the same outfit twice. Where does she get the money? And she only puts out the best wine, the best cheese and ham."

"From the sales. She sells everything. She gives it to us for free because she wants us to like the boy."

"She never said whose it was, did she?"

"Never: that's why people make up their own stories, and they aren't talking about god."

"That and the fact that María Teresa looks like a witch and her boy keeps getting weirder and weirder."

"Did you see that nasty shit he has out in the yard?"

"I couldn't look! It makes me want to vomit."

As the moms entertained themselves with hands of cards, we tried to make up games that Julito could participate in. It wasn't easy: Julito didn't understand anything, he tore up cards, broke the rules, and immediately went crying to his mom that we were leaving him out.

The moms would shout at us without lifting their eyes from their cards—"Play with Julito, dammit!"—and when we complained that he didn't follow directions they held up their hands with their cigarettes to shut us up.

The only fun thing about Julito was seeing him play with his leeches.

There was a baby pool in the backyard filled with fat black leeches that were Julito's pets. Our mothers had forbidden us to go in the water no matter how hot a day, but Julito would strip naked and let the leeches stick to his body. Nothing made him happier. He would laugh and clap, and drool would drip down his chin like some translucent insect.

His fearlessness was the only thing that made him better than us.

After a while in the water Julito would stand up and show us his white body covered in black leeches. It was his superhero costume. Maybe because it was the only thing he did that we wouldn't do, he used the leeches to frighten us. He would pull one of those gross creatures from his nipple or his thigh or his crotch and fling it at us. He loved to watch us run away in terror, disgusted, feeling imaginary leeches all over our bodies, as he posed with outstretched arms under the sun and laughed hysterically, like a god of the underworld.

From the spot where a leech had been sucking on him a trail of blood trickled down his body in slow motion, staining his belly, his monstrous feet.

One day he threw a leech at my face and I felt its needlelike mouth stick immediately to my cheek. I ripped the slimy, disgusting thing off me and without thinking twice I threw it down and stomped on it as hard as I could: red blood stained the sole of my shoe. Julito transformed into a savage beast. He threw himself at me, fully naked, covered in leeches, and began to attack me.

With his gigantic tongue, those thin, black little teeth, he got in my face and shouted the only insults he knew. The sound of his voice, hoarse, guttural, choked with rage, is something I'll never forget.

"Spawn of Sa-tan. Bas-tard. Spawn of Sa-tan. Bas-tard."

He came at me with such force that I tripped and fell into the little pool. Immediately the leeches began to unstick from the walls in search of my flesh. The other kids pointed and laughed at me just like they laughed at Julito. Suddenly he was me and I was him. I stood up shakily and launched myself at Julito like a blind, rabid, evil animal.

I wanted only one thing: I wanted to kill him.

Julito sickened us, Julito was dead weight, Julito was stupid and dumb, Julito let his blood be sucked by those nasty creatures, Julito's mom thought he was made of sugar and honey.

I wasn't.

The moms came over and broke up the fight. Mine grabbed me by the hair and screamed at me. She'd been drinking, so she was more violent than normal. She hit me in front of everyone and called me a monster: "I don't know what to do with you, you little monster." In contrast, Julito's mom wrapped him in a towel, patted his corn-colored hair, and kissed him on his huge, veiny head.

In the car I scratched my neck and discovered another leech. Disgusted down to my bones, I threw it out the window and imagined Julito throwing himself under the wheels of the car trying to save it and being flattened and his stinking blood staining the cement for a long time, for all of eternity, and everyone who walked by would tell their kids that this was where the ugliest boy in the world had died.

I smiled.

My mom asked me to tell her what happened, so I told her the truth: "Julito threw a leech at me."

"Look, I know that kid is like something out of a horror movie, but you have to be nice to him, do you hear me? You have to treat him nice for your mommy. Promise me. If you fight with him, María Teresa is going to be mad at me and then your mommy won't have anywhere to play cards and she'll have to stay shut inside the house all the time. You know I'm not happy when I'm at home, don't you? You know how angry I get if I have to spend all day shut inside the house, don't you?"

The next time I went to Julito's house there was no debate over what to play.

I suggested hide-and-seek.

Julito only had two hiding places: behind the door to the guest bathroom and inside a broken refrigerator in the storage room. No one made much of an effort to look for him. He could stay hidden for ages, sometimes we forgot all about him, and when we said goodbye his mom would ask where he was and we'd have to pretend that we'd just started playing.

"I found you, Julito."

He would clap and squeal with joy and try to give us kisses with his slobbery mouth.

That day he hid in the old refrigerator. We made eye contact. I put my finger over my lips. Don't worry, I won't tell anyone, Julito.

I left him there. Every once in a while we'd shout,

"Julito, where are you? Where are you, Julito?" We could hear his nervous little laugh from inside the appliance.

Then we forgot all about him.

It was an incredible afternoon that went on forever. We played soccer, ping-pong, Monopoly, races, video games. We ate cookies and drank Coca-Cola. Julito had all the toys in the world, and he didn't play with any of them. Everything was gnawed on, drooled on, sticky and half-broken by his twisted hands. We pretended they were our toys and that we were privileged, beloved children.

When it came time to leave, Julito's mom asked us where he was. We told her that we were playing hide-and-seek, and she smiled.

"Let's all look for him," she said, and she kissed our hands and thanked us for being so kind to her little boy. We paraded through the house, calling out to Julito. His mom shouted that his friends were leaving, that the game was over, that he was the winner, that she'd made his favorite cookies. Julito was nowhere to be found. She searched the whole house, her face getting whiter and whiter, her voice shakier, her body rigid as if someone were pointing a gun at her.

"Julito, my love, come out, you won, come out and we'll give you a prize."

The moms opened closets, looked under the beds, in the dirty-clothes hamper; someone went out to the baby pool to see if he was maybe splashing around in there but found only the black leeches stuck to the walls, waiting for some live creature to fall in.

As we were checking behind the curtains in Julito's room, my mom grabbed me by the arm so hard her nails drew blood. She said I knew where Julito was hidden and that I had to tell his mom immediately. I shook my head.

"You know where he is, you little bastard, I know you know."

"I don't know, I really don't know."

"When we get home I'm going to tell your dad to give you a beating."

I rubbed my head in the spot that the belt buckle had hit me last time. I told her Julito's two hiding places. When I mentioned the refrigerator she went pale and her eyes opened wider than I ever knew eyes could open. She uttered three words.

"You killed him."

Right at that moment we heard a scream that sounded like the earth opening up, like the wail of an ambulance, like an explosion, like thunder right on top of us. I don't know if I imagined it, but the entire house seemed to shake, the lights swung from the ceiling and the glass in the windows cracked. It was a sound like all the beasts of the world howling in unison, like the enraged ocean. A scream like a total eclipse.

INVADERS

The neighborhood where my family became a family wasn't always what it is today. And neither were we.

There was a time in which us kids would play in the half-built houses, all bare cement, exposed rebar, and stairs with no railing. We would climb mountains of gravel and sand from the construction sites piled up on every corner and pretend we were astronauts on a new planet until they called us to dinner.

It was the start of everything, the start of our lives and the start of that city, maybe of the entire world.

Every once in a while someone would stop to ask for directions to such and such address. It was impossible to answer with any certainty because there were no street signs or house numbers; only the deeds to the properties could provide any real information. My parents knew that ours was number sixty-six, and our neighbors on either side were sixty-five and sixty-seven. That's it. Beyond that it was a maze of construction and everything else all around us, beneath us—wetlands.

The inhabitants of that new neighborhood were all middle-class, between twenty and thirty, with one or two kids, paying in installments, employees of some large company, wearing clothes Made in China, dreaming of trips to Disneyland.

One day my father drove us in his brand-new red car to see the house under construction, and even though the smell of saltwater and rot prevailed, we would soon be the ones to prevail over the wetlands. "Don't worry," he said. "That's the smell of the swamp dying," he said. "The city has to grow," he said. I couldn't imagine how we could be stronger than the wetlands, a live creature with a dozen tentacles hugging the city from north to south, a conflu-ence of the raging river where drunk people drowned and the bodies of outspoken workers were disposed of.

But my father was sure that a monster made of flesh was stronger than a monster made of water.

So we moved. The first night a huge rat climbed up through the toilet, and Dad, with a broom in his hand, sent us to bed saying it was the Tooth Mouse; he'd heard there were new kids here and wanted to meet them. After that, every time one of us lost a tooth we hid it from our parents as long as possible: we didn't want that black wet thing that lived in the sewer burrowing under our pillows.

Every day on the sidewalks we encountered bewil-dered iguanas, mutilated, gnawing at some piece of garbage like toothless old women. The frogs that tried to cross the road got run over by cars over and over again until there was nothing left but a thin amphibian veneer, a vague outline.

We once saw a group of crabs emerge from the wetlands. They skittered up the steep street like a squad-ron of little red tanks trying to frighten the enemy with toy pincers and creepy rotating eyes. A truck carrying construction materials drove by and crushed them with a loud crunch. One red pincer kept slicing at the air even after the little crab lay in pieces on the asphalt.

Herons landed in the fresh cement thinking it was mud, looking for worms or larvae, and got stuck, to the delight of the cats and dogs who gnawed at their bones and spit out their cottony feathers. It was almost unbearable to watch the birds walking delicately over the trash piling up on the street corners. Like little girls in filthy tutus, too beautiful to live among so much shit.

One of the first things Dad bought for the house was a bug zapper. All night long, every few seconds, we would hear the crackle of electricity and we knew that a fly, a mosquito, a moth, a lightning bug, or a flying cockroach had been reduced to a small corpse. The lamp was indifferent, impartial, killing dragonflies as well as mosquitoes, ladybugs, and fireflies who maybe, dazzled by the light, thought it was their mother. It even zapped the little Australian parakeet that my parents bought us in the market for getting good grades. We named him Lorenzo, and he was turquoise and yellow. My sister called the light the Electric Chair, and sometimes when it zapped a big enough moth, we could smell the horrible stench of burnt hair and flesh. Someone told us that the bugs weren't trying to commit suicide: they simply thought the light was the moon, so they flew around it trying to reorient themselves and then got burned.

All night long we listened to the music of insect death. Sometimes, when I thought everyone was sleeping, I crawled under the mosquito netting and turned off the lamp. After a few minutes Dad would miss the sound of whipcracks and turn it back on. Immediately, the electrocuted creatures would begin to crackle.

At first there were so many crickets, millions of them, that they would darken the walls, ceilings, floors. The whole night reverberated with their unbearable chattering in the backyard, between the folded clothes, in the bathroom, in the linen closet, or from inside some shoe.

And there were other horrifying sounds besides the Electric Chair singeing the bugs and the din of the crickets. In the rafters lived entire extended families of bats who at night became the true owners of the house. Shrieks, wingbeats, scratching, and little sucking sounds could be heard in the early morning hours. Out of the bat shit grew tiny worms that would fall through the cracks in the ceiling and land on our beds, our desks, our colorful rugs, our dollhouse.

When it got too unbearable, when we woke up covered in bat-shit worms and the smell coming off the roof was nauseating, Dad would call the exterminator to fumigate the roof with poison. I pictured the sleeping bats ambushed by that murderous air. I imagined them hugging one another as they fell like black flowers, dead. After a few days the exterminator would come back to sweep the mounds of bat corpses into black garbage bags.

Childhood was fear, poison, infestation. Us and them.

At six o'clock every evening the fumigation truck passed by to bathe the houses, and whoever happened to be in the front yards, in a cloud that smelled like guayaba, vinegar, and ammonia. They would announce over a loudspeaker that we were supposed to open the windows and let the smoke inside, but Mom would close them because the smell made us cough and cry and left our eyes bright red.

They started to move in little by little: one family at a time, at night, in silence. They made their houses out of cardboard, scrap metal, and pieces of discarded wood. Some could afford paint, but others left the raw materials exposed: walls made of signs for some presidential candidate, a refrigerator or bicycle box, rice sacks, a tiger-striped blanket. They cooked their food on little fires outside the houses, and the kids, some carrying babies, ran around everywhere in packs, laughing, followed by a dog, always a dog.

No one taught us this, but when we came face to face with those other kids, them and us, we immediately put our guard up. Maybe it was that our pets wore collars and theirs didn't. Maybe it was their bare feet, our shoes. Maybe it was in our eyes, the mutual stares.

When it came to kites, however, we were united. Other things besides bats, flies, crickets, mosquitoes, could soar the gray skies of that city, and when they did, the air was clean and the day was filled with cheering, with love for those colorful pieces of paper on the wind.

Us and them gazed up at the same sky.

One of those kids decided he wanted my brother's kite one afternoon, the monarch butterfly, and even though he was smaller, he was very strong, or who knows, just desperate to fly it. A woman ran over, ripped my brother's kite out of the little boy's hand, slapped him, and tried to give it back to us, but the damage was done. My brother had already crossed the street crying and was ringing our doorbell like a madman, shouting about how they'd stolen his kite, his monarch-butterfly kite.

My dad charged out of the house like a wild animal released from a cage: ready to kill. He started shouting to anyone around who would listen that those people had to go, they were thieves, that the invaders had gone too far, the miserable lowlifes were mocking us. The neighbors rallied around him, applauded.

"You're the only one who can help us."

Dad was emboldened by those words. When he responded he was no longer himself, but someone a little taller: the chosen leader.

"All right, neighbors, I'll fix this. Leave it to me."

That night Dad called his cousin, the politician, and the story of the monarch butterfly kite became the robbing of a bicycle at knifepoint, my brother's face beaten and left with a busted lip and a black eye, the danger, the constant fear, the invaders who had converted our idyllic middle-class neighborhood into a no-man's-land bereft of god and law. A neighborhood in which the unthinkable was happening: homeless people were taking over plots of land and living there, as if they'd paid for them, as if they had some right.

The cousin called the mayor, mentioned the word *elections*, and the next day, even though it was a Sunday, they sent in the bulldozers.

Dad walked among the crowd like a king wearing a guayabera. The only thing missing was for him to be lifted up onto a platform, but that wasn't necessary because he was already floating several meters above everyone else.

His cigarette like a torch, his satisfied smile, his protective hand on the shoulders of the little white children, group hugs. He repeated his last name for people, answered their questions, raised his head.

"Yeah, I have some contacts."

Bulldozers are toothy, roaring beasts out to destroy everything in their path: person, animal, or thing. They rolled in one after another, like alien spaceships, onto the land that the families had occupied and began to tear it all down.

The screams from inside the makeshift houses were apocalyptic.

I pressed my hands to my ears with all my might but I could still hear their cries deep, deep, deep down, so deep I wanted to scream too.

Before the eyes of all the neighborhood, watching as if it were some street performance, the half-dressed women clutched their babies to their chests and with their free hands dragged along the bigger kids who looked back at what had been their lives, their eyes wide at the nightmare of it all. The men tried to salvage mattresses, clothes, utensils, rescue elderly people who couldn't walk. They shouted, everyone shouted, like when there's a bombing scene in a war movie.

Sheet metal, cardboard boxes, pots, and hammocks were catapulted through the air by the bulldozers, a mess of dust and objects that moments before had been the homes of those kids and their families. And the neighbors' applause in chorus with the horrified shrieking. They clapped for the bulldozers and clapped for my dad, who with his mouth said, "It was nothing, it's my civic duty," and with his face said, *Yes, I have saved you, you losers, love me and adore me because I have saved you.*

Then a little boy ran up to the brutal machine. Some say he saw a kitten, some say he saw something shiny, they all say he wasn't right in the head. The metal shovel gobbled him up as if he were an ant, with terrifying ease. His skinny little body flew through the air and fell almost soundlessly onto that hodgepodge of brick, wood, cardboard, and stone.

We all saw it happen. The man driving the bulldozer saw it. His mother saw. The woman crumpled to the ground with a deathly howl and began hurling fistfuls of sand into her eyes, ripped at her hair, scratched her chest until the flesh hung in strips, the blood staining her flowered dress, her sandals. The neighbors, confronted with the scene, grabbed their children and hurried to their homes without a backward glance.

Mom tried to stop Dad, but he shook her off violently.

"What? It's not my fault those people are so stupid."

He turned to head home, but someone called out to him. The mother of the boy, with a voice like thunder, said my father's full name.

He tensed, his back to her.

She repeated his name over and over as if she were throwing daggers. Then she spit in the dirt and wiped her chest, her nose, and her eyes with a single movement of her arm. Her face was still bloodied.

Dad kept on walking. When he got to our front door he shook his head, pulled a cigarette from the pocket of his guayabera, and muttered as he put it in his mouth, "Fucking witch."

That winter was brutal. It rained so hard that the toilet, sink, shower, and drains overflowed and transformed our house into a cesspool containing the whole neighborhood's shit. We all got skin infections that made our hands and feet blister. Mold stained the insides of the closets blackish green, our teddy bears mildewed, our shoes cracked and peeled, our clothes, closets, even us, all took on the stench of a wet dog.

The street disappeared under the water. The bolder neighbors waded into it, unable to see anything past their thighs; some went out in canoes or with plastic floats to try and save the stray dogs or take some food to the elderly residents. From the second-floor window we saw all kinds of trash float by: bottles, doors, dead animals, strollers, bouquets of flowers, fruit and vegetables.

The winter lasted a century, and when it ended, when the sun finally came out and began to dry out our lives, we were changed people.

Many decided to move to the higher part of the city. We couldn't. Dad owned land and livestock, but he'd lost everything, absolutely everything, to three months of rain.

So we began the times of buying on credit at the store and eating only rice with scrambled egg or tuna, bologna and cheese in wax paper, day after day. They moved us to a cheaper school; we were humiliated whenever they called us into the office to say our parents hadn't paid tuition. Every once in a while we said goodbye to yet another family leaving the neighborhood, promising to stay in touch. We girls would all cry hugging one another and the boys stared at their feet, not really sure what to do with their sadness or with the ever-shrinking soccer team.

That's how we grew up, like so many, losing.

One day, without understanding how it had happened, we realized that we didn't know anyone in the neighborhood anymore. The people who organized the block parties with speakers and kiddie pools on the sidewalks didn't even know our names. And we didn't know theirs.

Them and us.

We were the pariahs.

Where the invaders had lived, hundreds of houses sprang up, crowded together like crooked teeth. They opened beauty parlors, internet cafés, pharmacies, stores selling pirated DVDs and cheap home goods, evangelical churches, daycare centers, doctor's offices, immigration lawyers, veterinary clinics, salsa clubs, and restaurants.

Dad came home from work every day cursing under his breath. He hated the new neighbors' music, their colors, their decorations, their food, their devotion, and their noise. He called the police every weekend and not once did the police come out. At first, when he was still young, he would knock on the doors of the houses where the parties were being held and shout at them to turn down the volume, that didn't they know who they were dealing with, that he would call the police, city hall.

At first the neighbors told him to relax, invited him in for a drink. Then they started to insult him. Finally several boys came out of a party, stood side by side, very close together, staring him down, asking if he wanted trouble.

After Mom died us kids all moved away. She was the glue that held us together, the hinge. Without her, everything stank of gas and filth; without her we were like kites without a string, floating aimlessly on the wind.

The measure of the distance between a family is the measure of a family's pain.

We heard that thieves had tried to get into the house from the back patio and that Dad had decided to surround the place with barbed wire and alarms. He cemented the front door shut, boarded up almost all the windows, turned the house into a gray box, a coffin. In there, all alone, reliving who knows what memories.

Every day he woke up to find an extra six had been scrawled beside the street number sixty-six, and every day he'd paint over that added digit using leftover paint, throwing murderous glances at anyone walking by. One day, fed up, he stopped doing it and the address became 666.

The children feared him. Our home became the haunted house of the neighborhood, and they whispered that Dad was a cannibal, a pedophile, that he'd killed us all, that he was the devil. His appearance was proof enough. Dirtier and dirtier by the day with his shaggy white beard, his super long nails, he was feverish with hate, muttering curses and talking to himself about other, better times, when it had been a nice neighborhood, a community of decent people, not drug addicts and foreigners.

When we called he told us about the dark faces that appeared in the second-floor windows and said, Die, you shitty old man, about the threatening letters slipped under his door, pictures of bullets with his name written on them, how they threw rotten eggs at his house, spray-painted graffiti and inverted crosses on his wall, that the whole neighborhood threw trash at his door, that they cut down the tree in his front yard and used it to make a bonfire where they burned an effigy with a white beard and a cigarette in its mouth.

In our last conversation I no longer recognized his voice. He whispered into the phone that they were inside the house, that they were in our rooms, in the kitchen, and that soon they'd make it to the bathroom, where he'd been hiding for days, not eating or sleeping. I asked him who—again, like I did every time—I asked him who had come into the house. He always had the same response.

"The invaders."

PIETÀ

He's so dizzy he can't walk straight. That car like a spaceship parked crooked in the garage. He wobbles when he gets out and I take him by the arm, but he pulls away angrily because he's too proud, always has been, ever since he was a little boy, and he drops his keys by accident, he'd never throw them at me, he has manners, he comes from a good home. I bend down to pick them up off the ground. He's so handsome, his honey-butter hair, always so clean with his clothes ironed perfectly, sweet smelling, a prince crossing the garage, but it looks like he's about to trip so I lean forward with my arms out ready to catch him, just in case. This is how the whole world behaves around him. Everyone is always at his beck and call even before he's opened his mouth. Poor thing, he tries to talk, not realizing his tongue is dancing all over the place, thinking he's an adult and not a little boy learning to speak. I taught him to speak myself. It took him a long time, longer than my son, for example, who from very little could say mama, papa, milk, water, and everything else babies say to make themselves understood and make themselves loved. But he didn't and so I started talking to him all day, telling him things about the adult world and the baby world all mixed up together, anything and everything that popped into my head, about my neighborhood and the problem with the sewage system, about this white-carrot puree, how yummy, about what a huge mess the rain makes near my house with trash and dead dogs floating down the street and how we have to walk through that water to get to work, the rat infestation, that we need to get a cat, a fat, greedy cat, just anything. He would stare at me with those big blue eyes of his and it felt like being looked upon by Baby Jesus, like the Christ Child was watching you, and one day when I was complaining about the price of rice, he said *ice*. He meant rice, he said rice, and I screamed louder than if I'd seen the Virgin perform a miracle, but I didn't say anything to Señora because the señoras are jealous of us and she might've fired me for teaching the boy to do what she couldn't or for teaching him to say rice, a servants' word. Who knows. Anyway, I kept it to myself, but he soon started pointing to things and naming them. As if he'd just been waiting for permission and I'd told him the day before to talk—go ahead and talk, my boy—that no one would ever try to keep him quiet because he was the king of the world and he could say whatever he wanted, he could make it up: we would learn his language. The first time he said mama he was referring to me, not Señora. And that day I felt like I was flying, like I was floating above the earth. My beautiful boy, who wouldn't fall at his feet? That little pink mouth and porcelain skin. He hung on my neck, cried when I tried to set him down so I could clean the house. He clung to me like a little monkey as I swept the floor and folded the clean clothes. He was like that for a while: hanging on to me without ever letting go and Señora when she saw that would grab him from my neck but he'd throw such a huge tantrum that she had to let him come back to me. My son from the time he was a little baby would be all peace and quiet when I went to work and a neighbor looked after him, as if he knew, you know? Like he had to grow up quicker. But not my little boy, he wouldn't even let me go to the bathroom alone and sometimes I had to do my business with him holding my hand, like a little animal. I'm nervous now and he slaps me to calm me down but I don't say anything because I know he's not doing it out of meanness, it's just that he sometimes has a few too many drinks. It's because of those friends of his he runs around with, they're bad people, they take advantage of him, offer him who knows what. He accepts out of politeness. I taught him to say please and thank you. Señora told me not to teach him certain words and expressions that I used and that were things another kind of person would say, not a boy like him. Señor was also one to hit the drinks too hard and those kinds of things can maybe be passed down. Señor was terrible when he came home dizzy, ay, better to hide and keep out of his way. I would bring my little boy into my room when I heard his father come home because Señor would knock down anything that got in his way. I've never seen that kind of violence in anyone. I'll never forget the day the dog, Bobi, started barking for whatever reason. The dog was already old, half-blind, he couldn't hurt a fly. A little saint, my Bobi, my old man. I raised that dog from the time he was a puppy, tiny, so little he could fit in my hand. That was back when Señora was having a hard time getting in the family way, so Señor bought her a little puppy to distract her from all the doctors telling her that she was the one with the problem, that Señor's parts were working perfectly, even though Señor never did any tests that I know of. I was so ashamed when I got pregnant that I didn't say anything until it got to the point I couldn't hide my huge belly anymore and she saw me and said, "You're going to be a mother, how nice." For years Señora tried to get in the family way, she did all the treatments, I gave her the shots myself, poor thing, but no luck. And then the house felt like some haunted house in a movie, so much crying and wailing, you felt sorry for her. That big house without any children, you know? What a waste. Then they went to adopt my little boy from another country because, as Señora said, it would be strange for people so white like them to have a dark little baby, like the people here, and my little boy on the other hand was perfect, as if he'd come straight from her womb, because Señor's great-grandfather, the one who was president, had been like that: white-skinned, blond-haired, blue-eyed. White-skinned-blond-haired-blue-eyed, Señora would say. But, anyway, before that we were so happy when he brought that dog home. Señora told me that he was pedigree, the son, grandson, and great-grandson of purebreds, but the truth is that Bobi acted just like the mutts in my neighborhood: he chewed up shoes, ate garbage, stole meat from the table, and we had to hit him on the snout with a newspaper. He ate special food that cost more than they paid me on account of him being pedigree, as Señora told me. But then, well, what had happened was one day Bobi got it into his head to bark at Señor but Señor had been drinking and he kicked the dog in the stomach so hard that the dog just went like *hmmmf* and went stiff. My boy wanted to go see what had happened to his dog and I drove myself crazy trying to distract him so he wouldn't see. I had to make something up. I didn't know how to explain it to him. So I lied and said Bobi had gone to heaven because he was so old and I had to console that poor little boy crying a river of tears because he'd grown up with that dog, they'd grown up right alongside each other. It was so cute to see them together, my Baby Jesus and his loyal companion like on the pamphlets handed out at church. The missus as soon as she found out flew to the mall and bought him a new dog, super expensive, a beautiful little puppy, but my boy didn't take to it, he actually mistreated the creature, left him limping. I'd be washing the clothes and I'd hear the animal whining and I knew that my boy was doing something to it, not out of meanness, just out of curiosity, he was always so curious and sometimes he just wanted to see what would happen if he burned ants or stomped on birds. They ended up giving that puppy to me and my son fell in love with it immediately: he named it Bobi, after my little boy's dead dog that he'd heard me talk so much about and he wanted his own Bobi. It was around that time the doctor told me my son wasn't right in the head, that he had something wrong with him, degenerative, he said, chronic, he said, and Señora paid for him to see the neurologist, super expensive, just so that he could take one look and say the same thing, degenerative and chronic, the worst words in the world. He prescribed him some pills that he had to take for the rest of his life so he wouldn't have his fits, poor thing. Years and years that good little dog lived with us, very loyal. When Bobi died my son slipped into a depression there was no pulling him out of. My boy is shouting for me to help him. He's using vulgar words, because of his nerves. He tries to pull Miss Ceci out of the car but she's in a bad way herself, she looks like she's asleep, passed out. Ay, that girl, may god forgive me, I never liked her: spoiled, rude, with that high-pitched voice ordering my boy around to do this and stop doing that. And always wearing those tiny dresses, boobs hanging out, super high heels, that blond hair that Señora says is faker than a fifteen-dollar bill, those long nails. Ay, no. With so many pretty girls, from good families, out here and in the city too, all crazy about him. No, I never liked that girl for my boy, but once they're grown up you can't say anything. When they're little, it's different, they do everything you tell them, but once they're big they want to decide for themselves and if you dare to comment they'll shut you right up and put you right in your place, which is in the kitchen. I think he liked that it drove his mother crazy when he brought Miss Ceci home, oh, Señora would get so mad she wouldn't leave her bedroom. Has that woman left? she would ask me. And I'd have to go check. Sometimes I would hear them doing things in my boy's room and I'd die of embarrassment because for me he was still that baby hanging from my neck like a monkey. No, Señora, Miss Ceci is still here. I was terrified he'd get her pregnant, probably what that sneaky girl wanted, to get a baby out of my little boy and set herself up for life because boys like my little boy aren't a dime a dozen, he's one in a million, or even rarer. He yells for me to help him get Miss Ceci inside because she's, as they say, out of it. But even between the two of us we can't move her. He sends me to get the wheelbarrow. We toss her in like a sack of potatoes. The girl feels ice-cold when I touch her because my boy always has the air-conditioning on full blast in the car. He doesn't like to sweat and he has no reason to sweat. Son, I say to him, son, what happened. He doesn't answer, he's too worried about getting Miss Ceci into the house and checking to make sure no neighbors are watching. When he sees that I'm flustered and I don't know how to help, he yells at me, says horrible things, that he's going to kick me to the curb like a stray dog, that he's going to tell Señora that I'm a thief, that he's going to kill my crazy son who's a drain on society, but he just says those things because he's in his cups, I know he adores me, sometimes I think he loves me more than Señora, so I don't hold it against him, I just keep pushing the wheelbarrow with the girl splayed out inside, who knows where she lost her shoe. When the automatic light turns on I see the girl's face and that's when I let go of the wheelbarrow and my jaw drops to the ground and I cover my face because even though I've never seen a dead body I know that's what a dead body looks like. Son, son, what happened, son? The light blinks on and off, off and on, and every time it lights up the girl's face it looks worse and worse. They've massacred her. One of her eyes is mush, her nose drips dried blood, her mouth is swollen. Son. He tells me to shut up, says he has to think, and I stand watching him and I see that his shirt is stained. He looks at his hands, covered in blood, and that's when I start talking to him like when he was little: Come here, my sweet boy, come here and I'll make it all better. I guide him in through the service entrance. I lay him down in my bed, take off all his clothes, clean his body with a wet washcloth, rub him down with cologne, put antiseptic cream on his hands, caress his blond curls, and sing to him until he falls asleep like a baby. Don't worry about anything, my baby, I'll take care of you, I tell him. Then I put his bloody clothes in a pillow-case so I can take them to my house. My son is about the same size.

SACRIFICES

"Where was it? Green A?" he said as they looked for the car in the gigantic mall parking garage.

"Um, don't ask me. You're the one who said you'd remember," she answered.

"Green, definitely Green, I'm sure of it. A or B? Do you remember?"

"Dammit, this happens every time we go to the movies."

"Because they do everything backward! They use these stupid symbols and shit, impossible to remember. Do you remember the Galápagos?"

"How could I forget looking for that fucking Sea Lion F for half an hour."

"At least here there are colors."

"Yeah, but we're still lost like idiots."

"Hold on, I don't think it was on this level. Wait, this way. Let's look for a security guard to ask."

"Hit the car alarm button to see if we can hear it."

"Everybody else is gone."

"They're all geniuses, capable of remembering both a color and a letter! They're all so smart. Must be nice."

"This isn't funny."

"I'm not joking! I'm just saying that there are people who have a talent for this kind of thing and others who don't."

"Green, it was definitely Green."

"Is there anyone we can call?"

"Where's the elevator? The car's not on this level."

"Are you sure?"

"I don't know, why don't you look for it, Superwoman. I'm sure you'll find it right away."

"Don't start. Not now."

"Yes now, yes now. What's up with you lately?"

"Ugh, we better find the car fast, this is too stupid. I'm not about to fight with you right now."

"You won't even look at me, we always have to go to the movies because you can't even look me in the eye."

"You really want to talk about this now? Right now. I can't believe you're starting with this bullshit."

"Well, I am starting with this bullshit! I'm starting with it because you're always so pissed off and blaming everything on me! Why didn't *you* bother to remember the color and the letter? Because you have Mr. Moron here who has to remember everything, to take care of everything."

"What are you talking about? What are all these things you're supposedly taking care of?"

"The kids, the bills, calling the bank to raise the limit on your card, constantly walking on eggshells so that you, the girl made of Venetian glass, won't get mad."

"I can't believe you. You and your bullshit can just stay here. Bye."

"Wait."

"What?"

"Have you seen the elevator?"

"I don't think there is an elevator."

"Are you sure? What about stairs?"

"I haven't seen any stairs. You should look, fucking Sherlock Holmes."

"Hold on. Calm down. It has to be around here somewhere."

"Hmmm."

"This is Red R. How did we get to Red R?"

"We must've gone down."

"No, we didn't go down."

"How do you know? Then Red and Green are on the same level, I guess."

"But the car's in C."

"You said it was A."

"I think it was C."

"But you said it was A."

"It's C!"

"Well, we're in R. I can't believe we've wasted so much time on this bullshit. Can anyone hear me? Security! Please, we need help!"

"Should we call someone?"

"There's no signal."

"You're kidding."

"I'm serious. I don't have any signal. Check yours."

"I don't either."

"Seriously? You're joking. Let me see. Shit."

"Let's try over here."

"Did you get any?"

"Nothing."

"Fuck, they make these fucking parking garages worse and worse, like some maze, for real. I hate them."

"It's your own fault for not writing down where we left it. There's no one around because every other person is more than capable of remembering two goddamn pieces of information."

"And there she goes again . . ."

"Listen, we've been walking around this fucking parking garage for at least twenty minutes. How is it possible we haven't found the car yet?"

"Oh, you're right. Look, there it is: she who asks, receives. What part of I *don't fucking know where it is* do you not understand?"

"The part where you're completely useless and the part where why the fuck did I marry you."

" . . ."

"I could be sleeping peacefully in my bed right now, but no. I'm suffocating in this sweltering, gigantic fucking parking garage where my extremely forgetful husband isn't able to find our fucking car. Everyone and their fucking mom has found their car except for one single idiot!"

"In good company."

"What does that mean?"

"You're right here with me . . ."

"Security! Hello! Is there anyone here?"

"The mall is closed."

"What?"

"I tried to go ask a janitor or someone at the movie theater and the door was locked."

"Security! Help!"

"I'm sure they'll make their rounds through the parking garage before they lock up for the night."

"Yeah, they can't lock up without checking to see if there are people in here, right?"

"Do you see any stairs?"

"There are no stairs on this level."

"There's no emergency exit?"

"I thought I saw a sign somewhere."

"There's a wall."

"A wall."

"How is there only a wall? This is unbelievable. Fucking crazytown. I'm going to sue these people."

"Let's just start over, okay? This is ridiculous."

"We left the theater through that door and we turned to the left?"

"It was Green."

"Right."

"Could it to be the right? Because this is Blue."

"Are you sure?"

"I'm not the one who's color-blind."

"Just shut up. I'm sick of your constant insults and how every word that comes out of your mouth is just to throw some more shit in my face."

"Don't tell me to shut up. You're a shitty, shitty, shitty person."

"You are. You're unbearable."

"Where did you go last weekend?"

"What?"

"Answer me. It's a simple question."

"Into the city. To give that course. Why do you ask questions you already know the answers to?"

"Uh-huh."

"I think I heard something."

"I don't hear anything."

"Listen. It's an alarm."

"Where?"

"I feel like I'm hearing it from different directions."

"It's the echo."

"There it is again."

"Over there."

"I'm hearing it more from over here."

"I'll go over here, and you go over there."

"What if we lose each other?"

"Let's see, what color is this? Yellow?"

"Yellow H."

"It was nowhere near here, right?"

"There are no cars left at all."

"When did everyone else leave?"

"While my wife was in the bathroom for two hours doing fuck if I know."

"Now it's my fucking fault? Like you're so perfect."

"I watched as everyone left and you were still in the bathroom. I was about to go in after you."

"Why didn't you, if you were so worried?"

"Hello? It was the ladies' room."

"I was crying."

"I thought so. Why do you drag me to see these tear-jerkers. All boo-hoo-hoo. The husband left her. Boo-hoo, the new guy doesn't love her. Waa, waa, waa. So fucking stupid."

"You agreed to come."

"Then you sit there crying and crying."

"You came."

"It's called masochism."

"We've already been here, haven't we?"

"Doesn't look familiar to me."

"I can't believe there's not a single car left."

"Except ours. I'm starting to doubt whether we even drove here. Can you imagine if we'd come by taxi for some reason and here we are, walking around looking for our car like complete idiots?"

"That would never happen to me. That's the kind of thing that happens to guys who walk around with their heads up their asses, too distracted by who the fuck knows what."

"No, of course not. You're Little Miss Perfect."

"Perfect, no—just honest."

"What are you trying to say?"

"Where were you last weekend?"

"In the city, dammit, what the fuck, at the New Talent Training Center downtown."

"Wow, good cover story. You figured out all the details."

"What are you going on about?"

"You really tied up all the loose ends! Did you make up the address or find it on Google?"

"I don't understand, and to be honest it's so ridiculous I don't care. I'm just saying, I don't know how *you* feel about it, but *I* don't feel like this is the time to fight about made-up bullshit when we've been wandering around a parking garage for ages and we have no fucking clue where our car is."

"What did you put in Google? New Talent Training Center? Or did you make that up too?"

"Oh my god."

"Don't drag god into this. Fucking liar."

"Unbelievable."

"Or better yet, maybe you *should* drag god into it, to forgive you for being such a liar and such an asshole."

"Unbelievable."

"What's unbelievable is how you can even look at me with a straight face. Wait, this is A."

"But it's Purple."

"Is it possible you left it in Purple A?"

"No."

"No or *no*?"

"Mmm, *no*."

"You're not sure, see?"

"Stop fucking around, dammit. The car isn't here. It doesn't matter if I'm sure or not."

"Someone stole it."

"What?"

"That's it. How did I not figure it out sooner? Someone stole the car, they took it, it's not here!"

"Shit. But it was in Green."

"Stop with the *it was in Green, it was in Green* bullshit. Someone stole our goddamn car."

"But I have the parking ticket."

"*Ihavetheticket, Ihavetheticket.* Moron, the carjackers are probably working with security or they make fake tickets or who knows what they do. There's no safe place left in this shitty, shitty city. Nothing's safe in this fucking city! Security! Someone help us!"

"Relax. We'll go down and find someone to talk to."

"We can't find the elevator or the stairs."

"We'll climb out a window if we have to. Come on,

don't sit down, come on, let's go. We're going to find a way out of here, you'll see. Stand up, honey, come on. We'll laugh about this later."

"Don't talk to me like that, fucking cheater."

"We'll be out of here in no time."

"Don't touch me, don't touch me."

"What's wrong with you?"

"Where were you last weekend?"

"What is it with you? In the city."

"You weren't in the fucking city, you weren't, you weren't, you weren't."

"Yes, I was. Why are you being like this?"

"Ever heard of the Imperial Hotel? Huh? Sound familiar?"

"Stand up, let's find the car."

"If you touch me again I'll kill you, you fucking liar. I'll scratch your eyes out."

"Let's go find the car. This is no time to start believing bullshit gossip."

"There's no better time and no better place to talk about your bullshit."

"Get up."

"Let go."

"Get up."

"Let go of me, you monster."

"What do you think you're going to do? There's no one here. No one can hear us. What are you going to do?"

"What do you think you're going to do to me?"

"Fine, stay there. I'll go find security."

"You still claim you were in the city?"

"You're still going on about that?"

"What are you going to do to me?"

"What happened to the lights."

"Shit."

"Use your cell phone light. What does it say there?"

"There's a B."

"B for bullshit."

"Have we been here already?"

"Oh, for the love of god, we're never going to find the exit in the dark."

"How long have we been in here?"

"It's almost three in the morning."

"Security! Please! Someone help us!"

"You're going to lose your voice screaming like that."

"Security! Help!"

"I'm almost out of battery. What about you?"

"You or your phone? I have battery."

"We're going to have to sleep here on the ground."

"We have no choice."

"I hope the kids aren't waiting up for us. Carmen must be worried sick."

"I was thinking the same thing."

"This is fucking insane. I can't believe we've been in this parking garage for hours and we haven't seen a single way out."

"I feel like every time we walk by the same place it's a different color and letter."

"That's impossible."

"It's insane."

"It's a nightmare."

"Maybe it is."

"I already pinched myself several times."

"Hit the car alarm button again."

"Why?"

"To see if we can hear it."

"I think it's that way."

"We already went that way."

"Let's go again."

"Wait."

"What? Let's go, what are you waiting for?"

"Wait, listen to me. Every time we go by the same place it's a different color and letter."

"No, it just seems like it, but it's not."

"It's different."

"It's not. It can't be. We're just exhausted."

"I've been taking notes on my cell phone."

"We're just turned around. We've been walking around forever."

"It's not a parking garage."

"What the hell is it then? A maze?"

"They change."

"Come on, stop saying silly things and get up, let's go. I think I heard it over there. Push it again."

"Shine your light over there. What does it say?"

"It says O."

"Do you remember I just said it was B for bullshit?"

"It's not the same wall."

"It is the same wall."

"You're tired."

"Yeah, but it says O."

"We're probably going down without realizing it. See? Every time we walk around we're going down, but in these modern buildings you can't tell."

"It's O."

"It can't be."

"It is. And it's the same wall."

"Check if you have signal."

"I haven't had any signal since we got in here."

"Just check!"

"I'm running out of battery too."

"Fuck! No signal?"

"It's O."

"This can't be happening."

"Check the ticket. Maybe there's a phone number."

"We don't have signal."

"Then let's look for one of those emergency phones to call security."

"I've been looking for something, anything on the walls for hours. There are no windows, doors, faucets—just flat wall. With absolutely nothing."

"What's that letter? Shine your light over there. What does it say?"

"It's P."

"And the color?"

"Orange."

"It was Light Blue I before."

"Stop saying that, it's ridiculous. What does it say there?"

"'Don't forget the color and letter of where you parked. Thank you.'"

"It makes no sense. Help! Security! Please!"

"Listen."

"What?"

"I heard something, stand up."

"What? I can't see anything."

"I wish I'd never fucking quit smoking. We'd have a lighter at least."

"Shhh. Listen."

"You're right."

"Do you hear that?"

"Uh-huh."

"It's your cell phone, someone's calling! You have signal!"

"No. It just died."

"Shit. Shit. Shit. Shit. Fuck. Motherfucker. Shit. Shit. What are you laughing at?"

"I've never heard you say so many bad words."

"You've never seen me locked in a parking garage with no way out."

"We're trapped with no phone, no light, no car, no water."

"It's punishment."

"For what?"

"For your lies and your deception, because you've been out whoring around."

"Has it ever occurred to you that maybe it's because you act like such a bitch? Because all you do is scream at me all day long? Because you're always too tired, you have a migraine, you have dinner with the girls?"

"It's all my fault. Right. *I'm* the one who threw you into the arms of that latest slut they saw you with at the Imperial Hotel. Poor thing, he's so lonely and misunderstood by his bitch wife that he had to find some nasty tits with brown nipples to make him feel better."

"Shut up. Come on, let's keep looking for the exit."

"Answer me."

"We have to get out of here. I'm starting to feel bad, like dizzy."

"Answer me. Do you love her?"

"I don't know. She listens to me, she holds me. I don't know, sometimes I think I do. She's sweet. But then there's you, the kids. Hey, do you hear that?"

"Yes."

"What is it?"

"It sounds like someone's coming."

"Thank god, thank you, thank you, thank you."

"Where are they?"

"Sounds like they're somewhere over there, right?"

"Should we call to them?"

"Maybe. Hold on, no. Let's wait."

"They're coming this way."

"Yeah, it has to be a security guard, but let's wait for them to get closer."

"Why don't we call them over so they don't leave?"

"Wait."

"What's that sound?"

"Sounds like a dog."

"A dog or a pig."

"A pig, right?"

"Shhh. Don't talk so loud."

"It's coming closer. It sounds more like . . . a horse? A cow?"

"Fuck me, that's insane."

"It's creepy."

"Don't worry. It's probably a weird ringtone or a walkie-talkie. It's fine, it's not a horse, it's not a pig, it must be some joke. Should we call out to them?"

"Shhh."

"It sounds like some animal."

"Turn on your cell phone."

"It's going to make noise."

"Turn it on. I need to see what it is."

"What is that?"

"It's . . . it can't be—it looks like a bull."

"It's a man in a costume."

"No, it has horns and hooves. It's not a man."

"Then what is it? What else could it be? What kind of game is this?"

"It's coming closer."

"It's not a man."

"What is it?"

"I don't know what it is. But it's coming straight toward us."

EDITH

Who will grieve for this woman?
—ANNA AKHMATOVA, "LOT'S WIFE"

After making love, he always dozed off.

Then she could watch him at her leisure, observing his chewed nails, the gray hairs on his chest, his flaccid cock, glistening like it had been slathered with butter, his feet like two long palm fronds, and his forehead relaxed, finally free of that constant furrow that made him look as if he were trying to solve some puzzle with the sun in his eyes. She found it impossible to sleep with him beside her. That would mean missing out on the chance to openly observe him, not out of the corner of her eye but fully taking in his reddened nipples, his belly button filled with fluff, his bony shoulders, his lips letting out little puffs of air, a whistle in another frequency. She would've given her life for that little thread of hot breath, for the callus on his right hand where he held his tools, for the curve of a single one of his eyelashes. She would've given her life for him. It wasn't because of the sex. Or maybe it was. Because of the sex. What is sex? Meeting, rubbing up against each other, expelling viscous liquids? No. What is it then? Like having your back rubbed when you feel alone and you don't know what's wrong with you. Like a kid being picked out as special among all the other boys and girls. Like hearing someone say that you do it, that you do anything, better than anyone else. Like a kiss on the forehead. Like a friendly hand reaching out to guide you to shelter in a sandstorm. Like someone hiding a delicious candied fruit behind their back as a surprise for you. Like being someone else: not a woman married to an elderly man, mother of two girls, taking care of everything, carrying the weight of the world on her shoulders as if life in her own home didn't already weigh enough. A nomad and a slave mute to what her husband liked to do to her daughters.

Without opening his eyes, he slipped his arm around her hips to grab her ass and they lay there like that, a man and his lover's ass: this is mine. She was always wet for him, a warm jellyfish, a joyous anemone in its submarine cave, a lustful mystery. He would start out giving her long licks from her perineum to her clitoris, a tongue made of mercury or of eucalyptus candy, maternal and rough, pleasure banishing all her fears. Licking her worries away. Fucking to keep from killing herself. It felt like every embrace she'd ever craved and every sexual encounter she'd ever desired. He wasn't a man using his tongue, but a goddess cleaning her newborn babe. Sex as a return to the mother's womb, to preconsciousness, the pure pleasure of forgetting that you are a mortal fool. Sex as a happy home where flowers bloom.

Sex as all the words that we ever wanted to say but lacked the language for.

The first time he licked her clean like a bitch licks her puppies, she thought she would die, and she did. After the shock of pleasure, the struggle to enter and embrace the light, the explosion that both gives and erases all meaning, everything went black and the stars came out and the air filled with the smell of firewood as she wallowed in a dense, slippery mud more luxurious than any material on the planet, her nipples transforming into diamonds, and without even opening her mouth the entire world obeyed her command: the orgasm's legacy. Who wouldn't want to feel like that? *This is heaven*, she thought, and she died and came back to life blooming like a flower, begging to be crucified again, splayed wide. All door. *Here, here, come in here, please, have mercy.* Meteor showers in her belly, the savage sensuality of being fucked with desire and feeling desired: fucking and being fucked back.

During orgasm he said her name: Edith. He was the only one who said her name over and over with his tongue, with his sex, moaning Edith, Edith, Edith. She was no longer wife of, mother of, daughter of. She was that name that her lover repeated in his ecstasy, flooding into her every orifice. She was that woman named Edith and therefore she existed.

After coming, if he'd asked her to execute unspeakable acts she would have done it, anything, obedient as a dog. The drug of choice was cock, was tongue, was his name.

After coming, no one existed, nothing.

Every time they met in the little shepherd's cottage their desire transformed them into animals. When they ran out of ways to enter each other, they bit, scratched, brayed, spit in each other's mouths and pulled each other's hair, they locked eyes, held each other's pubic hair in their mouths and pulled at them with their lips, tried out strange positions, they laughed and cried. The most refined and the most primitive: an angel, a king, a barbarian, a coyote. When that man fucked her, she felt like she'd been born to open up before him, that her thighs had been made to press into his skinny back and suck him ever deeper into her like a tornado, farther in, into her house.

She knew that while she was lying on her back with her pussy twinkling, screaming in orgasm, with her eyes rolled back and her legs spread open like someone about to give birth, her husband was showing his old cock to their little girls. She didn't just suspect it, she knew it. Would anything have been different if she were there? Would she have been able to offer herself, like a sacrifice, in exchange for her daughters? Probably not. But perhaps the girls could take refuge in her arms, cry out their terror, believe for a few hours that their mother had some power, that it would never happen again. She could almost see them with their little legs skinny and white as powder, their delicate little crotches dripping blood, their tanned faces streaked with tears. Yes, she could've been there to console her daughters, but she had no choice in the matter: while her husband was occupied groping the bigger one and making the little one watch, he wouldn't be wondering why she hadn't come back from the fields and where the hell his dinner was.

Violence was the only constant in her life. The only certainty hour after hour, day after day. Unfailing. When she discovered sex with this man, her thirst was quenched and also magnified. One day they were both lying on the ground and, with her throat raw from so much moaning and screaming, she said to him, "My husband does monstrous things to my daughters while I'm here with you." He sat up and with the gentleness of a mother he wiped her vagina, her weak legs, removed the blades of grass from her tangled hair. Then he dressed her. He gave her a kiss on the forehead and he left without looking back.

Days passed without hearing his song outside her window like a bird that was not a bird. Without him no one ever said her name, and without a name she felt like a blank space, a ghost, a waste. She searched for him in crowds, at the market, at the seashore, in the whorehouses where the men all groped her with their eyes. She asked and asked after him until her voice was raw. She checked the leper colony and the temples and the taverns filled with bandits. She even searched for him beyond the wall, where the exiled wailed like babies and witches sold incense to ward off the evil eye.

No one had seen him.

Her husband waited for her to fall asleep, then slipped into the girls' bed. One night she was dreaming of her man. He smiled at her, ran to her, touched her all over, and she fell apart in his hands, turned to water, to light, to wind. She entered him through his eyes, his ears, his mouth, the sweet eye of his cock, through his ass where she gave him loving kisses. He inhaled her and drank her. She woke up in the midst of orgasm, soaked with her wetness and tears, half-crazed.

She found her husband lifting the sheet under which the little one slept, and she threw herself at him, ready to tear him to pieces, to cut off his head, his arms, his legs, his disgusting cock. He knocked her to the ground. A bloodstain spread across the dirt floor, and she lost consciousness just as the girls began to attack him.

When she awoke, she was on the back of a mule. Her hands and feet tied. Behind her was her village, the brown dirt and the golden sun of her childhood and the shepherds' hut where she'd met god. Behind her were her daughters, gravely wounded, barely alive, being cared for by the women of the temple.

Her husband held a whip in his hand, and he lashed the mule to make it go faster. Desperate with terror, she realized what was happening. She tried to scream, but he had gagged her. She tried to break free, but the knots only tightened when she moved. He spoke.

"If you look back something terrible will befall you."

She knew that she was leaving behind everything that belonged to her, her memories, her daughters, the cup she used to drink tea, and him, the only one living among so much death.

Then she heard the bird that wasn't a bird. His song like millions of stars exploding in the night. How could she not look as the sky burst open violently? How could she not look as god appeared before her?

She turned her head and there he was, her man, smiling and stretching out his hand to her.

"I warned you not to look back."

A feeling of intense warmth spread through her heart before she felt her body begin to freeze from the inside out. The pain was excruciating. She was left petrified, immobile as all the blood of her body ran downhill, returning, returning.

FREAKS

Look at the clock. Watch the big hand move until it reaches the twelve. Squeal because it's time to go. Run to the family minivan and climb inside. Dodge your brothers' punches. Ignore them saying fag, gay, queer boy, sailor boy, little fairy, big fairy, pillow biter, pretty boy, pansy, poof, nancy, sissy, pussy, wuss, dick licker, powder puff, homo, queenie until they get bored. Lift your head and feel the wind change, become purer, prettier. Smell the sea in the distance and smile. Dodge more punches. Listen once again to why are you like that, stand up for yourself like a man, what are you doing with your hand. Hug your grandmother. Eat dead fish so fresh its eyes are still gleaming. Run to the beach. Run like a dog. Run and run as fast as your legs will carry you. Dive into the water. Squeal with delight. Bathe in the foam. Sink into the deep. Hold your breath for so long that you feel like air is no longer necessary. Go down deeper and deeper. Touch the starfish, the coral, the sea turtles grazing like armored cows. Beg for a little more time in the water. Give in. Dry off. Eat lunch. Take a nap. Wake up red from sun and heat. Visit the town market and the circus. Go into one of the tents and see the bigheaded kid for the first time. Scrunch your nose at the smell of shit. Cover your mouth with your handkerchief. Hold back the bile that pushes the undigested fish up into your chest and makes your eyes water. Look at the boy with the big head, get a good look. Be seen by him. Ask what's wrong with that boy, why do they have that boy in there with the pigs and the pigs' mess, where are that boy's parents. Grip your mom's hand in fear. Break the bigheaded boy's gaze. Look back to see him crying, holding out his little arms to the people who stare at him. Repress a gag when a pig first sniffs the bigheaded boy and then shits on him. Shoo away the flies. Hear Mom say poor thing, and Dad say that's brutal, and your brothers, fucking disgusting monster. Insist that someone has to help him, to call the police, to get him out of there. Shout. Understand that no one, none of the adults who stare at the bigheaded boy in disgust and hold their noses, are going to do anything. Hide your tears as you see that the bigheaded boy, after crying and wailing, is falling asleep with a filthy thumb stuck in his mouth. Feel fury over being too small to wade through the muck to pick him up, give him a bath and then something to eat. Refuse to leave. Get punched on the shoulder by one of your brothers and pushed by the other. Listen again the whole way home to the string of insults that starts with fag. Have a dream in which the pigs eat the bigheaded kid, then the dead boy screams at you, asking why you didn't do anything, chasing you down the beach, wobbling on ridiculously small legs compared to the size of his head, a crab-boy. Wake up drenched in sweat and trembling. Dodge your brothers' punches as they ask if the little girl was scared by his nightmare. Watch them do an impression of what they think a scared little girl looks like. Remain silent. Get up at dawn. Help your grandmother make breakfast. Collect the eggs among swirls of feathers and angry clucking. Thank your grandmother for the coins she gives you. Eat breakfast studying your family members' faces. Watch the bread vanish into your brothers' jowls within seconds. See Dad's forehead, always so wrinkled, behind the newspaper. See the sad way Mom holds her teacup. Exchange a look with your grandmother who knows, who understands, who says I love you without saying a word. Run to town. Find the drunk who guards the entrance to the circus. Drop your grandmother's coins into his grimy palm. Recoil at his black-toothed, depraved smile, his tongue hanging out, his quick hand that tries to touch you. Enter the pigsty where the bigheaded boy sleeps. Shoo away the pigs, who shuffle off oinking. Pick him up in your arms. Feel surprised by how little he weighs. Hold him against your body. Smile. Run past the drunk, who shouts where are you taking the monster, if you want to do something to him you have to pay extra. Reemerge in the sunshine with the bigheaded boy in your arms like a proud mother with her baby. Leave behind the circus and the drunk man shouting for someone to stop the little fag who's stealing the bigheaded boy. Run to the cliff whispering that everything will be all right, that you're both going to be all right, that it's all over, all that horror, the pigs, the disgusted looks, the punches, the fear. Reach the edge with the circus people at your heels, shouting what are you doing, stupid fag. Look at the bigheaded boy smiling with his toothless mouth and his little gleaming fish eyes and without speaking he calls you brother, brother. Jump into the sea. Feel the fall as your legs entwine and merge into one, transforming, quickly and violently, into a tail that slaps the water, churning up an iridescent spume, blinding in its beauty.

MARÍA FERNANDA AMPUERO is a writer and journalist born in Guayaquil, Ecuador, in 1976. She has been published in newspapers and magazines around the world, and is the author of two narrative nonfiction titles and the short story collection *Cockfight*, published by Feminist Press in 2020. In 2012 she was selected as one of the 100 Most Influential Latin Americans in Spain.

FRANCES RIDDLE has translated numerous Spanish-language authors and was the recipient of an English PEN grant in 2021. Her translation of Claudia Piñeiro's *Elena Knows* was shortlisted for the International Booker Prize in 2022. Her work has appeared in journals such as *Granta* and the *White Review*. Originally from Houston, she now lives in Buenos Aires.

More Translated Literature from the Feminist Press

The Age of Goodbyes by Li Zi Shu,
translated by YZ Chin

Arid Dreams: Stories by Duanwad Pimwana,
translated by Mui Poopoksakul

La Bastarda by Trifonia Melibea Obono,
translated by Lawrence Schimel

**Blood Feast: The Complete Short Stories
of Malika Moustadraf**
translated by Alice Guthrie

Cockfight by María Fernanda Ampuero,
translated by Frances Riddle

Grieving: Dispatches from a Wounded Country
by Cristina Rivera Garza,
translated by Sarah Booker

In Case of Emergency by Mahsa Mohebali,
translated by Mariam Rahmani

Panics by Barbara Molinard,
translated by Emma Ramadan

Sweetlust: Stories by Asja Bakić,
translated by Jennifer Zoble

Violets by Kyung-Sook Shin,
translated by Anton Hur

The Feminist Press publishes books that ignite movements and social transformation. Celebrating our legacy, we lift up insurgent and marginalized voices from around the world to build a more just future.

See our complete list of books at
feministpress.org

THE FEMINIST PRESS
AT THE CITY UNIVERSITY OF NEW YORK
FEMINISTPRESS.ORG